Praise for Path to Pas...
"Path to Passion is a jour...
some snarky humor and s...
romance. I highly recommend it." ~ Felicia Denise

"Exciting and captivating." ~ Maya Love

Praise for A Perfect Caress
"Ms. Prah did a wonderful job bringing the atmosphere and ambience of Italy to life and I will admit they were among my favorite scenes in the book." ~ Debbie Christiana

"Sweet and fun and passionate." ~ Love Bites and Silk

Praise for the Destiny Series
"Incredibly addictive and soaring with heat." ~ Lucii Grubb

"Beautiful writing, fabulous character development, and hot and steamy love scenes! I love it!" ~ Stephanie Sakal

"Nana is entertaining and thought-provoking." ~Diana Wilder

ALSO BY NANA PRAH

Destiny Series
Midwife to Destiny
Destiny Mine
Entwined Destiny
Destiny Awakened

The Astacios
A Perfect Caress
Path to Passion
Ambitious Seduction

Others
Love Undercover
Love Through Time
Healing His Medic

Nana Prah

his Defiant PRINCESS

3

First Published in Great Britain in 2018 by
LOVE AFRICA PRESS
103 Reaver House, 12 East Street, Epsom KT17 1HX
www.loveafricapress.com

LOVE AFRICA
~ PRESS ~
African Love Stories

ISBN: 978-1-9164755-5-7
Also available as eBook

ACKNOWLEDGEMENTS

Thank you to my fabulous readers. You're all the best!

A huge thanks to Kiru Taye and Empi Baryeh for allowing me to be part of the Royal House of Saene series. My literary sisters are amazing and I am just happy to tag along with them on this wonderful adventure.

As always, I thank Zee Monodee for being the absolute best editor to work with. With her there is only growth, growth, and more growth for me as a writer.

A grand-stand thank you to Love Africa Press for publishing the #RHOSaene Princesses's stories and taking the initiative to bring more African romance to the world.

Long live Love Africa Press!

.

To Maame Aba Yorke, your support means more than I can ever convey.

CHAPTER ONE

Jake Pettersen had flown over five thousand miles from Vermont to West Africa to see someone he'd met online. On a social media site about superhero movies, of all places.

Was he crazy?

Sure, the conversations he'd had with Amira over the past year had left lasting impressions, leaving him contemplating issues which had never crossed his mind before. She had a witty personality that made him laugh out loud in public places. It had been impossible to resist her beauty and elegant mannerisms.

So why was he afraid of meeting her face-to-face for the first time? What if the woman he'd come to know and respect turned out to be an illusion? Or worse, a disappointment. He'd built her up in his mind as perfect. Or at least, perfect for him. What if she wasn't?

A year of daily communication should've equipped him with the ability to get to know the real her. Not even a method actor could be that good at hiding their true self for so long.

His best friend and business partner, Calvin Shepard—always up for an adventure—had decided to tag along. Now that they'd landed, Jake was glad he hadn't travelled alone.

The 'fasten seatbelt' sign switched off. He unbuckled himself from the economy seat and waited for his turn to disembark.

Calvin shifted to the aisle. "Ready to meet the woman of your dreams?"

Jake tilted his head from side to side, eliciting the popping sounds that made others cringe. How could he answer? Was she the woman for him? He'd developed feelings for her, but how would he recognize if she were his? The questions threatened to give him a headache, and yet, his mind had never once revolted at taking the journey.

His synapses fired with the exhilaration of being so close to meeting her in person. Whether Amira was the woman he was meant to be with for the rest of his life or not, they were great friends, and that settled any nervousness he may have had.

"I'm ready to meet my friend."

Calvin chuckled. "You didn't drag me all the way to Africa to meet a *friend*."

"I didn't drag you anywhere." Jake pointed to the front of the plane, indicating for Calvin to follow the others. "You jumped into my damn suitcase mumbling something about Africa being a place you had to visit before you died, and then begged me to let you come with me."

"Funny how two people can have such different memories about the same event," Calvin tossed back over his shoulder.

They walked along the tunnel leading to the large international airport and exited into the inner dome where they waited to get through the surprisingly long line at immigration. Before he'd started talking to Amira, he'd never heard about the African country of Bagumi. He hadn't expected so many foreigners to be visiting. Amira had mentioned that it was a popular tourist area, but it was easier to see it than just imagine.

Calvin hitched the strap of his carry-on bag higher on his shoulder. "And yet, here we are. On a spontaneous trip, all for love."

"More for a meet and greet."

Calvin rolled light brown eyes skyward.

"Spare me, Jake. You can at least be honest to yourself." Calvin drove him forward with a slap to the shoulder. "Be willing to accept what happens with Amira. Here's to hoping fireworks blow up the roof, and you'll have found the woman you're meant to be with."

Leave it to his oldest friend to declare the ultimate truth.

His excitement rose once they'd gone through passport control, retrieved their luggage, and then customs before heading in the direction of the airport's exit.

They stepped out into a large lobby area where people waited with broad smiles and expectant faces. Up front and centre stood a dark-skinned man with a poster bearing Jake's last name.

Jake looked to the left and right of the man, expecting to see Amira's dark, almond-shaped eyes searching for him.

His shoulders fell in disappointment. Why hadn't she come to the airport to meet him?

As they strode towards the man with the sign, his expectations rose once again. Maybe she'd stayed in the car to avoid the crowd. But that didn't make sense because she loved being around people. How many times had he called her an attention-seeker when she'd told a story about always being the life of the party?

He extended his hand to the man holding the sign and spoke some of the few words in her language that he'd absorbed when she'd attempted to teach him. "Hello, my name is Jake Pettersen."

The older gentleman's eyes widened as his bushy brows rose.

"Hello. My name is Runako," he returned in his language with a smile. "I am your driver. Welcome to Bagumi. It is a pleasure to meet you," he continued in a rhythmic rise and fall of accented English.

"This is my friend, Calvin Shepard."

Runako nodded at Calvin. "Welcome to Bagumi. I am sure you will both enjoy your stay." He reached for Jake's bag.

Not accustomed to people carrying anything for him, he held on to his things.

"I'll take care of my own luggage." To soften the rejection he added in the dialect, "Thank you."

This brought a wide smile to Runako's face. "Please follow me," he said in English.

They did as instructed. The unexpected stifling atmosphere once they stepped out of the air-conditioned airport snatched Jake's breath away. The combination of the sun beating down so close that he swore he could touch it, along with the suppressive humidity made standing on the sweltering pavement a tortuous event for the short time it took Runako to open the car door.

Sliding into the back seat of the vehicle, he took in deep gulps of the cool air the running engine emitted. Amira had warned him about the weather, but he hadn't taken it seriously. He'd been to Cancun back in college and had survived. What else had she mentioned about her country that would end up testing him?

He looked over to see Calvin grinning and shook his head. "Didn't the heat bother you?"

"Not one bit." Calvin's laughter mocked him. "I'm not the idiot who flew to a country which nearly kisses the equator all trussed up in a suit."

Compared to Calvin's more laid back and cooler look of a pair of light khakis and a polo shirt, Jake had been the one to make a mistake in wardrobe. He'd desperately wanted to impress Amira with one of the few suits he owned.

He removed his jacket and tie, unbuttoned the top two buttons of his shirt, and rolled up his sleeves. He could only hope the sweat saturating his shirt would dry by the time they reached the hotel.

Runako pulled out of the temporary parking space, and soon, they found themselves in a city the likes of which he'd find in a large US state. The road was smooth as they whipped past skyscrapers creating the skyline.

After about fifteen minutes, the landscape shifted to a more suburban scene. The homes varied in size from mansions to moderate-sized. Jake rested his head against the seat and enjoyed the change in scenery as homes were replaced by thick copses of trees with occasional villages consisting of interspersed neat, cottage-type houses.

After an hour and a half, Runako took a left off of the main road. Thirty minutes later, a palatial edifice came into view as if they'd come upon a mirage.

"Welcome to the Palace of Bagumi," Runako announced with pride. "The home of King Saene and the royal family."

Jake shook Calvin's shoulder to wake him. What were they doing at the king's palace? "Will we be taking a tour before we're sent to our hotel?"

Runako caught his gaze in the rear view mirror with a quirked brow. "This is where you'll be staying."

His Defiant Princess

CHAPTER TWO

Amira Saene paced in her eldest brother's office. Zawadi, the next king of Bagumi, watched her for a moment, shook his head with a deep frown, and returned his attention to his computer.

Adrenaline wouldn't allow her to sit as she waited for Jake to arrive. When had her stomach ever been tied in such knots? As a princess, she'd been trained to remain cool and composed at all times. It would've been ideal for her nerves to remember that as she gnawed on her manicured nails.

Why hadn't she broken protocol and gone to the airport to meet him? Resisting her favourite treat of peanut brittle had been easier than forcing herself to stay in the palace to receive her guest as decorum demanded. It also might've made things easier if she'd told Jake who she really was, but she hadn't. The way he'd treated her like a regular person had kept her lips sealed about her status as a princess of a prominent country in West Africa.

She glared at Zareb, the youngest of her older twin brothers and the chief of palace security. When she'd requested permission for Jake to visit, she'd pleaded with Zawadi not to tell anyone about her relationship with him. Meeting someone on the Internet these days wasn't a crime, but she doubted her family would agree.

Zawadi had insisted on informing the hardest member of their family. She'd had to relent because of the current instability in Bagumi. The neighbouring kingdom of Ashani had become more violent with direct attacks on cattle herders over the past month.

Disputes over the water rights of the river between their two countries would lead to war if her father didn't defuse the situation soon. Although a smaller country, Ashani held a powerful army. Too many lives would be lost if they fought.

Zareb hadn't been happy about Jake coming into the country in the first place, but not even he had ever been immune to her charms, or incessant whining. Sometimes, being the youngest and the only female in her mother's line had its benefits.

"Amira, you will not speak during the questioning," Zareb ordered.

She pinched her lips together to keep from arguing. He wouldn't hesitate to fulfil his earlier threat of kicking her out of the office altogether. She gave a curt nod and strode to the window. Too bad Zawadi's office faced the back portion of the palace's extensive grounds instead of the front where the driver would drop off their guests. Maybe seeing him from afar would settle her racing heart.

She jumped as a knock sounded on the near-impenetrable Bubinga wood. Inhaling and then exhaling twice as long through her nose like she did while practicing yoga did absolutely nothing to calm her.

"Come in," Zawadi said.

His secretary opened the door. "Your Highness, the two guests you were expecting have arrived."

"Thank you. Please escort them in."

Amira swallowed the nothingness drying her throat. Every cell in her body vibrated at a higher frequency, and she swore she could've evaporated.

"Amira."

She pivoted her head towards the voice of her eldest brother. When had he gotten up to stand beside her?

"Sit down."

With stiff legs, she toddled to one of the gold and maroon armchairs across the room. As taught in her multitudes of etiquette classes, she lowered herself onto the seat and crossed her legs at the ankles.

The door opened again, and all composure bolted as she leapt to her feet. The man she'd gotten to know over the past year entered, sucking all the air out of the room. He strode past her towards the desk. The scents, sounds, and coolness of the room dulled as her vision, attuned only to him, heightened.

His commanding presence dwarfed her more than his six-foot, broad-shouldered frame did. How many times had she longed to run her fingers through his thick, light brown hair to feel if it was really as silky soft as it appeared while they'd chatted on Skype? She'd often fallen asleep thinking about his brilliant eyes which reminded her of light sapphires with subtle varying hues of blue within. Even on camera, the dynamics of his irises had been vivid.

A high forehead, sharp nose, strong jawline, and that luscious mouth. A full, pink bottom lip with a slightly thinner top one which she'd imagined running her tongue along. Her face heated at how far her imagination had taken her with this man.

And now, he stood in front of her and her brothers. The next king of Bagumi along with the most disciplined and strictest man in possibly all the world.

She sank into her chair with all decorum forgotten and prayed.

A sound from the corner of the room had Jake turning to see what his peripheral vision had glimpsed when he'd walked in. For a moment, he shifted his eyes away from the imposing men standing before him and spied a woman. His gaze flung back to do a double take, escorting his body with it as he stared at Amira.

He feared his already hyperactive heart would fail with the increased effort that seeing her had wrought.

The cream-coloured top tucked into a dark pencil skirt emphasized her slim waist and full hips with the added pleasure of highlighting her lovely brown skin. Her dreadlocked hair, normally flowing over her shoulders when they spoke, was now pulled into a high bun.

He couldn't take his gaze off of her dark eyes as something unfamiliar and undefinable struck him, making him ultra-aware of nothing but her presence as a strange longing flipped in his stomach. Without a thought, he took a step towards her.

His outstretched arm was restrained by a vise grip.

"Please have a seat, Dr. Pettersen."

The voice which penetrated his mind sounded muffled.

How could he be anywhere but close to Amira? She drew him to her, and he had no will to resist. What would it be like to finally stroke a finger along her cheek? To lean in and touch his greedy lips to hers and breathe in her scent? What did she smell like? Taste like? Never in his life had he had such a strong desire to absorb someone's essence into himself.

Distress at discovering the intensity of his attraction to her should've pushed him to run out the door. Instead, desire heated his skin and released gravity's pull, willing him to float closer.

16

Was she as mesmerized? Needing to touch? Or was it just his imagination?

"Jake."

He recognized Calvin's insistent voice as a hand waved in front of his face, obscuring his view of the most beautiful woman he'd ever encountered. He slapped it away.

"Our hosts want us to have a seat," Calvin said in a loud, slow tone.

Hands on his shoulders pivoted him.

As if he were awakening from a deep sleep, the room came through as hazy until he blinked several times. What had just happened? Shaking his head, he scrubbed a hand down his face. Maybe it had all been a vision?

Once he'd sat in the chair, he turned and found Amira standing where she'd been a few seconds ago. He stayed attuned to her as he forced himself to return his attention to the meeting.

Had the room been this tense when they'd entered?

The narrow eyes of the fierce man glowering down at him as if meaning to do harm did nothing to dim his euphoria. Instead, he focused on the less annoyed man behind the desk. The penetrating dark eyes reminded him of Amira's as he got the impression he was being analysed and judged.

"Dr. Pettersen and Mr. Shepard. My name is Prince Zawadi Saene, and this is my brother, Prince Zareb—" he paused and looked between him and Calvin, "—our head of security. Welcome to Bagumi."

CHAPTER THREE

Amira attempted to hide the empty feeling in the pit of her stomach by resuming her straight-backed posture.

She tried to pay attention to the interrogation her brothers were doling out to Jake, but couldn't. Her gaze kept wandering to the magnificent man who'd come into the room and possessed her soul. She'd never thought meeting him would elicit such an explosive energy within her.

What had happened? One moment, she'd been nervous with expectation, and the next, an award-winning gospel choir had sung as her being had been elevated to greater heights and Jake had become her world. The need to run to him had been blocked only by her family's insistence for decorum. But for those few moments, she would've gladly thrown away her regality for just a second of being in his arms.

Her body had craved it. Her nerves still hummed, sensitized, urging her to close the interminable distance between them.

She shook her shoulders to try to rid herself of the feeling. Just because nothing like that had ever happened to her didn't make it real. It must've been the anticipation of seeing him after their daily conversations. The initial sight of his knee-weakening handsome face just a few feet away where an ocean had separated them before had incited the absurd reaction.

What about the way he'd stared and extended a hand towards her before Zareb had restrained him?

"I insist that you not reveal how you met my sister while you're here."

Zawadi's words snapped her back to the conversation.

Jake's head tilted. "Who's your sister?"

Zawadi waved a hand in her direction with a look of annoyance. "Amira, of course."

Her blood ceased to flow as dread hit her. What had her brother just done?

This wasn't how she'd wanted Jake to find out about her royal status. She should've told him a long time ago, but she hadn't wanted him to treat her differently. People seemed to get irrational and behave with deference when they learned she was a real-life princess. She didn't want that from him.

Friendship had been her goal when they'd started talking, and then, it had transitioned into a potential relationship. He'd liked the woman he'd gotten to know, not what people generally perceived a princess to be.

He angled the top half of his body in her direction but kept his gaze on Zawadi as he pointed across his chest at her. "Amira is your sister?"

"*Princess* Amira. Of course," Zawadi stated in his most arrogant tone, as if the world knew it as a fact.

Only then did Jake give her his full attention.

Having been raised by a powerful queen, she held his gaze. She didn't flinch. A princess never did.

His eyes darkened as if a storm of incredulity had built up behind them. "How come you never told me?"

With her mouth poised to open and spill the truth, Zawadi spoke first.

"That is of little consequence here."

Jake ignored her brother. "Your father is the king?"

"Yes, but I'll never be the ruler," she answered with a voice that didn't quiver. "That honour goes to Zawadi."

"But why didn't you mention it?"

Was this a conversation to have in front of her highly protective brothers? She sighed and stifled the embarrassment that admitting the truth provoked. Squaring her shoulders, she maintained eye contact. "I wanted you to get to know me for who I am. Not who my family is."

"So you gave me a false last name?"

She winced at the harshness in his tone, which elicited a growl from Zareb. A warning for Jake.

"I didn't lie," she defended. "Oware is my middle name."

His knuckles whitened as he gripped the arm of his chair. "By omission, then."

She lowered her gaze. What could she say? Nothing. She had lied, but for self-preservation, not to be deceitful.

Zawadi knocked against his desk. "The rule stands. No one is to know how you met."

She understood the reasoning behind the edict, but doubted Jake did. With the uncertain unrest in Bagumi, no one could be trusted with information that may put the royal house in a negative light. Meeting a man on-line and then having him visit would seem extreme for the conservative people. Especially since she was their princess and had her supposed choice of men to choose from. Little did they know.

Expecting Jake to have questions, she was surprised when he nodded.

"I understand. Um, Your Highness," he tagged on as if remembering in whose presence he sat.

A sharp ache struck inside her chest. Why had he acquiesced without an argument? Did he truly comprehend the reason for her brother's request, or was he embarrassed about how they'd met?

"I'm sure Amira has told you about the recent insurgence escalating from a neighbouring country of Bagumi," Zawadi stated.

For the first time, she took direct notice of Jake's friend as he shifted forward with his neck extended in avid interest.

"Due to the threats, neither of you—" Zawadi paused to look at both of the strangers to their land, "—will be allowed to venture off the compound by yourselves. You will always have a guard with you."

She released her breath when the only reaction from the men was a nod. The danger outside the palace was real, and she'd be aggrieved if either of them got hurt while visiting.

Zawadi leaned back against his seat as if relaxed. She knew better.

"To be honest, I don't see why you're here. If it weren't for indulging the whims of my sister to make her happy, you wouldn't be. You possess nothing. No title. No wealth. You are a middle-classed foreigner working as a dentist. Not even a medical doctor with the potential to save lives." Zawadi scoffed, unleashing his elitism. "What do you have to offer my sister?"

Amira shot to her feet. "Zawadi!"

Face flaming, she turned to Jake who, with pursed lips and corded neck, looked as if he were ready to ram the desk into her brother and out the window.

She rushed to Jake's side and touched his shoulder in an attempt to calm him. To tell him she didn't care about wealth or titles.

And then, her world tilted as the power of their attraction catapulted into her, flinging her in a dimension that consisted solely of him. The tangy spiciness of his cologne filled her nostrils as tingles blazed up her arm. Heat settled at her core as the darkened blue pools of his eyes beckoned her to get lost within their depths.

"Amira."

She blinked at the call of her name and snapped out of her mesmerized daze. What was going on? Snatching her hand away from the potent heat of his body, she lowered her head, turned, and went back to her seat.

When had Zawadi moved to the front of his desk?

"I *must* have your word that you and Amira will be chaperoned at all times when you are together."

After witnessing their intense reaction, she didn't blame him for the edict; yet, it still angered her to the point of once again springing to her feet. How dare he treat them as if they'd strip each other naked the moment they were alone?

Zawadi spoke quickly. "I'm sure you'll understand that as royalty, we have our modesty to maintain. Just as it has always been, the daughters of the king cannot—" he shot a narrowed gaze in her direction, "—and will not, be found unchaperoned with a man who is not family."

She held back a snort. If only they knew how many times she'd snuck out with the few guys she'd dated. The explanation was weak at best. She waited for Jake to put up an argument.

After a few seconds, he said, "Yes, Your Highness."

She dropped into her seat as disappointment weighed her down. Had she lost him with the omission

23

of her status? Or perhaps, he'd never intended to have anything more to do with her than friendship.

Throwing back her shoulders, she shrouded the positive attitude she was known for. First and foremost, she and Jake were friends. If something more developed between them—which at that point, seemed more unlikely than her becoming the ruler of Bagumi—she'd deal with it. No matter what happened, she'd ensure that he had the most enjoyable two weeks of his life.

CHAPTER FOUR

Jake observed the artwork as they passed through the never-ending hallways towards where they'd be staying. The eclectic collection belonged in a museum rather than a home. There had to be pieces from all over the world gracing the walls, and he had yet to see what had been placed in the rooms themselves.

Assessing them kept him from turning to look at Amira. Correction, *Princess* Amira. She'd explained why she hadn't told him who she was, but the betrayal still stung. Why hadn't she trusted him? They'd gotten close, sharing things that not even his oldest friend knew. Talked about their dreams and aspirations. They'd become friends, so why couldn't she have told him?

Calvin shifted a little closer to his side and whispered, "I'm surprised they didn't send us an indoor cart to transport us to our rooms."

"At least, its air-conditioned."

He couldn't imagine how much they spent to keep the massive place cool. He chanced a glance back. Dark, slanted eyes caught his gaze, and his mouth went dry. He'd thought her beautiful when they'd video chatted, but in real life, she could only claim the term stunning.

They needed to talk. Alone. He returned his sights forward without looking at Zareb. The job as head of security suited his quarterback-shouldered tall frame. Intelligent, all-observing eyes made sure nothing got past him. As long as eagle-eyed Zareb wasn't his personal guard for their stay in Bagumi, he'd find a way to spend some alone time with Amira.

Slowing his pace, he maintained a parallel stride with her. "Princess Amira, are you really working as an intern for your family's business?"

The start of the conversation caught Zareb's strict eye, but Jake didn't care. No one had told him he couldn't speak to her.

She looked up at him with wariness.

"You can just call me Amira, and yes," she answered in the same sweet voice which had kept him up many nights talking. "I don't blame them, either, considering that everything I've done so far has been strictly academic."

Unlike him. He'd wanted to be a dentist ever since he'd learned what his mother did for a living. He'd started a practice with a few of his classmates, with Calvin being their business manager, and although it hadn't been easy going, at least, they were now turning a profit. "Experience is always a good thing to obtain."

They'd started their relationship when she'd been in Switzerland studying for her masters in business administration.

"I thought I'd be getting some at a higher level."

He shrugged. "You have to start somewhere, and the employees will appreciate that you earned your positions rather than them being thrown at you."

"This is your suite," Zareb announced.

Jake cursed the timing of their arrival. He had so many question. So much to learn. The most disturbing part of being around her was that he didn't want to leave her magnetic presence.

Zareb unlocked the door with a key card and stepped in, with Calvin in tow.

Jake hung back and looked into Amira's eyes. "We need to talk."

"Yes." She placed a hand on his arm, sharing a tingly heat that had his heart racing. "Listen, I'm sorry I didn't tell you about being a princess, but—"

Before she could finish, her brother's glowering eyes pierced them. "I'll show them their rooms, Amira. Don't you have to return to work?"

She sighed. "I start my vacation tomorrow."

"Are you sure your family owns the company?" Jake asked.

Her giggle caused goose bumps to rise along his arms. Delightful.

"I'll be off for the next two weeks while you're around." She cut her gaze to her brother before returning it to him. "Even with a chaperone, we'll have a wonderful time."

Did her softened voice sound uncertain? Had his reaction to the astonishing news of her status decreased her incredible confidence? He couldn't have that.

"Yes, we will." He held up the burner phone Zawadi had given him with the Bagumi number. "If it's okay with you, I can call."

Her full, glossed lips rose in a smile. "I'd like that."

He handed her the phone so she could input her number.

He stood drilled to the spot once she'd returned it. Not even the presence of her overbearing brother could force him to look away. How had he never noticed the tiny beauty mark in the right crease of her nose? Or the true lushness of her lips. His heart thundered, and the need to touch her overwhelmed, just as it had when he'd initially seen her.

"Dr. Pettersen, your room."

The deep bass voice snagged him out of his trance.

He turned to Zareb, keeping his expression neutral rather than growling at his insistent presence. "It's Jake, Your Highness. Nobody wears the name Dr. Pettersen quite like my mother, and I can't compete."

That got what appeared to be a miniscule lift of the lips from the man.

"Call me Zareb." He turned to Amira. "Work."

"Fine. Let me know if you need anything."

You, by my side. "I will. Have a good time at work."

"Thanks."

The slight shove from her brother sent her in the direction they'd just come from.

"Have a safe journey," Jake said in regards to the extended walk she'd have to make back to wherever she was going.

The comment caused both siblings to laugh. Jake almost collapsed at the sound coming from the head of security.

And then, tension flared as the stern look returned and Zareb stepped forward.

"Amira is my baby sister." How had his voice become even more ominous? "She deserves nothing but the best, and even if it takes my last breath, she will have it. Unlike my older brother, I know that it takes more than money and status to make her happy. If you hurt her…"

The words were replaced with a level glare that said it all.

So the man didn't mind if he wasn't rich, held no title or prestige. It wouldn't stop him from attempting to tear Jake apart if he didn't do right by Amira.

Refusing to cower, he held the prince's gaze. "I'll treat her like the woman I've come to like and respect. With honour."

The comment seemed to appease Zareb because after an intense stare down, he backed away and waved a hand into the room.

The three hours Amira had endured in the office before leaving had been useless. She hadn't gotten anything done because she'd been busy contemplating her encounter with Jake. Her body had kept in constant motion with both anxiety and excitement. If she wasn't wringing her clammy hands together, she'd been jiggling her knee, or pacing. Would he forgive her for not admitting her status?

If he didn't, he wasn't the man he'd revealed himself to be, and good riddance. At least, that's what her head rationalized. Her heart had her hands trembling while she chewed the inside of her cheek. She hated the reappearance of the nervous gestures she'd learned to control years ago.

She took the back routes to the guest wing once she'd returned to the palace so she'd be seen by few. She knocked on the door and slunk into the shadows to wait. No need to make it easy for Zareb's security team to find her since she'd made it that far without being caught.

When the door opened, she rushed forward and shoved Calvin into the room before closing it. He raised both hands and backed away.

She couldn't help the laughter. "I'm sorry, Calvin. I needed the quick cover."

"What's going on?" Jake said as he exited one of the suite's rooms.

Calvin rubbed a hand through his auburn hair and smirked "I was attacked in my own abode. I thought this place was supposed to be safe."

Amira giggled again. "Not from me."

"So I see." He held out his hand. "We haven't officially met. It's a pleasure to meet you, Princess Amira."

She grasped his hand and shook it. His dark brown eyes danced with humour. So it hadn't been her imagination when she'd observed them glimmer earlier in the day.

"The pleasure is mine. You are welcome to Bagumi. I will try my best to ensure that you enjoy your stay."

"I'm looking forward to it." He stepped back and glanced to the left. "I'll leave you two alone before I end up in a body bag."

Jake's thinned lips and narrowed eyes as he glared at his friend came into view as she turned her full attention to him.

When he looked at her, his features softened. "What are you doing here? Did anyone see you? Will you get into trouble?"

Was it nervousness that had him asking such rapid-fire questions? She could certainly understand because her palms were as wet as if she'd placed them in water.

"Playing hide and seek as a child has its advantages. I know this place as well as any of my siblings."

A thick silence hung between them. What else had he asked? She couldn't remember, and she didn't care. The giddiness of being alone with him sent blood whooshing through her ears.

Would jumping onto him and wrapping her legs around his waist be too forward? Her mother would be mortified, but then again, she wasn't there.

Jake stepped towards her with his arms open wide. Joy replaced doubt as she rushed into them.

She'd had no idea what to expect, but the exquisite melding of their bodies brought tears to her eyes. Clasping her arms around his shoulders, she stood on tip toe, bringing herself flush against him. His muscular arms banded around her, pulling her even closer as her stomach rode a rollercoaster of dips and flips that weakened her knees while heating her core.

She closed her eyes and took him in. Every contour of his body and his fresh soapy scent had her wishing he'd never let her go. And he didn't.

Not until Calvin's hushed voice intruded.

"Hey, you guys. Didn't you hear the door?" He looked between them as they peeled themselves apart. "Unless you want us to be discovered breaking the rules, which I'm personally against, I suggest that Amira get into one of the rooms."

Alert from the stupor she'd been entranced in, she pivoted to escape discovery. Before she could slip away, Jake grazed his lips across her temple. The area burned with the sweetness of his touch, and she planted her feet, ready for more of his caress. Without speaking, he turned her towards the direction from which he'd initially entered the living area and gave her a gentle nudge. She followed his silent order and went to hide.

Once Amira was out of sight, Jake attempted to calm his thundering heart by sitting in an armchair and breathing through the hands he'd cupped over his nose and mouth. Whatever had just happened between him and Amira had transcended anything he'd ever experienced.

He could've sworn his soul had glided into her and claimed her as his. Absolutely nothing else had ever felt so right. So far beyond extraordinary that he felt as if he were pulsating from head to toe. They would definitely have to explore their chemistry.

After they had their much-needed talk. He wanted her in his life. He'd known it after the first few months of their communication. Not a day had passed that they hadn't spoken at least three times a day. No matter how busy he was, he'd make time for her; otherwise, his day felt incomplete.

Love had bloomed, yet he'd never told her. The physical aspect of their attraction had still been a missing factor in the equation. Now, he knew for certain that Amira was the one he wanted to marry. His instincts and heart never steered him wrong. Ever.

Calvin opened the wooden barricade, and Zareb barrelled into the room.

Jake breathed out a frustrated sigh as he got to his feet. Would the man shadow his steps the whole time they were in Bagumi?

Zareb took a sharp look around the room. His nostrils flared with his deep inhale. "Amira come out here. Now."

What the hell? How did he know? Jake couldn't smell her once she'd left the room.

Amira walked out with her head held high. "We were chaperoned the whole time."

Zareb shook his head.

"Is that why you were hiding like a mole?" He turned to Jake, his lips pursed. "I came to check on your comfort and to inform you that dinner will be in two hours. The dress is formal."

Annoyance shone in his eyes as he glared at Jake. "I was going to send another of my security to escort you, but the job now falls to me. Come, Amira. Since you also need looking after, I'll walk you to your room."

For the briefest of moments, her shoulders drooped, and her eyes dulled. But then, the sparkle returned, and she smiled at Jake. She never let anything get her down for long, preferring to sit on the brighter side of life.

"What my brute of a brother forgot to mention was that this is our weekly family dinner. My father, both queens, and their children who are currently present at the palace will attend. Dignitaries, if we have any, will also join us." She raised a curious brow to Zareb. "Are there any?"

"Yes," came the curt reply.

His neutral expression made him difficult to assess, unlike Amira who allowed him to read her. Jake always knew where he stood, and that gave him a greater peace about falling in love. From what he'd learned, manipulation wasn't in her nature.

It hadn't taken him longer than the walk down the hallway to their suite for him to accept that her lie of omission hadn't been to hurt or deceive him, but as she'd mentioned in the office, to protect herself.

She came to stand in front of him and placed a hand on his arm. The area singed with awareness as she ignored Zareb's growl of disapproval.

"Don't worry about meeting the king. He's more down to Earth than either Zawadi or Zareb, and you handled them well."

Jake chuckled, but then sobered as he looked at her brother's stern face.

Zareb turned to leave. "Let's go. Gentlemen, remember that the rules are not just for your protection, but for my country's, as well. Abide by them, or suffer the consequences."

With her back to the door, Amira mocked her brother by twisting her lips and crossing her eyes, once again making him laugh even though he knew the man was serious. Jake had no desire to find out just what those consequences were, but neither could he stay away from Amira.

CHAPTER FIVE

Once a week, Amira's father insisted that his family sit together for a meal. It didn't matter if he was present at the palace or had travelled. When everyone was in town, his two wives, seven children, and the king ate as a surprisingly happy family. The wives behaved more like sisters than rivals, and their children were close. Amira's mother, Queen Zulekha, the first wife, knew her role as the most powerful and influential of the wives.

Being born the last of both her mother and father's children, Amira had been pampered by her large brood of a family. Her two sisters, Isha and India, tolerated her as only big sisters could—with continual torment. And yet, even they were protective of her when they felt it necessary, even if she didn't.

Guests were often added into the milieu. Because of her friendship with Jake, he and Calvin had been invited to the table.

Her hands trembled as she anticipated everything that could go wrong. Most of her siblings had become fun to be around once they'd grown past the teenager stage. Zareb could be a hard-ass, but at least, he meant well.

When she strode into the formal dining area, all eyes rose to meet her, but one pair of blue orbs caught and held her interest. Two hours had crawled by since she'd clung to him and felt the tantalizing caress of his lips against her skin. If only she had the power to contort time so this dinner would fly by and they could be alone together again.

"You're late, Amira," her mother stated with a slight frown marring her beauty.

Amira lowered her gaze, placed her hands on her upper thighs, and bent at the waist to show deference to everyone in the room before entering.

"I'm sorry, Mama." She left out the explanation of having to try on eleven different outfits. Her mother wouldn't care.

Head still bowed, she found her way to her seat. Isha, who always sat to her right, snickered so only Amira could hear.

She ignored her oldest sister as she settled in before lifting her head to find the source of her breathlessness.

India caught her gaze from across the table with a slight wave. Amira smiled at India's discrete thumb up as she flicked her eyes in Jake's direction.

"So it's true," Isha said.

Amira struggled to pull her gaze from Jake to look at her sister. "What?"

"You're attracted to the foreigner." At least, she kept her voice low so no one else could overhear. "A white, middle-class commoner, at that." She shook her head. "Even if the sex is mess-up-your-hair extraordinary, he's not worthy of a princess. Even you."

Her sister's tart tongue shouldn't surprise her, but her snobby attitude did. "Is it only money that makes a man worthy of a woman?" she hissed.

"No, but it helps. Especially when he has no status. But no worries, little sister." The condescending tone wasn't lost on her. "I'm sure this crush will pass, and then, you'll get on to finding a proper man. One just as handsome, but with a worthy stature. And money. Lots of it."

Nana Prah

Amira's heated retort was cut short as the person to her left spoke. "Hello, Princess Amira."

She stifled a snarl as she recognized the voice of the man who sat there. Instinct had her attempting to shift her seat closer to her sister who gave her a querying look.

Clearing her throat, she glanced up to see if anyone had noticed her reaction to Duak Omiata, the first born son of the king of Ashani. Her reaction seemed to go unnoticed by the others, but when she met Jake's gaze, his eyes had darkened to a stormy bluish-grey as the tanned skin of his face reddened.

She pasted on a smile to dispel his obvious anger, but he wasn't looking at her. Duak, who had leaned closer and grasped her hand, held his contempt.

Duak's voice scraped along her skin like the cheap acrylic sweater a kind friend had given her for Christmas in Switzerland. "You are as beautiful and succulent to the eyes as ever, my darling Amira."

Her body gave an involuntary shiver of revulsion, and she struggled to swallow the bile burning her throat. Snatching her fingers from his, she clasped her hands together as she maintained a polite façade to the vile prince. "Good evening, Duak."

He frowned at her intentional lack of his title, but she didn't relent. She refused to sit next to the wretched man throughout the meal and went to push her chair back. Her father getting to his feet stopped her from moving.

The room went silent.

"Tonight, we are honoured to have invited guests in our midst. We all know Prince Duak from Ashani." He paused to allow everyone to acknowledge Duak with a nod. "Dr. Jacob Pettersen and Mr. Calvin Shepard are from the United States of America. Be

37

gracious to them, and let them experience our inexhaustible hospitality."

Her family smiled at their visitors. Jake's lips remained downcast as he stared at Duak. Could he tell how much she detested the prince? Or did he have his own innate sense of when someone was vicious and rotten to the core?

For the sake of her father and not embarrassing her mother, she decided to maintain a civilized deportment. How could she get out of sitting next to Duak without causing a scene?

The answer came a moment later when her father sat after making a few more announcements.

"Your Majesty," Jake addressed the king. Everyone froze. Just as when her father had spoken, not even a server moved.

"Yes."

"I would be most humbled and pleased if you would allow me to be seated next to Prince Duak." Had he snarled the name? "Since I won't be travelling to his land during this visit, I would enjoy hearing about it directly from someone who has grown up there."

She lowered her head and hid her smile behind her fingers. Jake had sensed her discomfort, and just like a true hero, he'd stepped in to save her. How could she not love him?

A sense of disorientation made her grip the edge of the table. Yes, she truly did. She'd fallen for the personality she'd come to know during their easy conversations. What hadn't she learned about him? They'd discussed everything from toothpaste preferences to their stances on corporal punishment. His family was as familiar to her as her own, even though she'd never met them. She understood his motivations. Best of all, he knew her as a woman, not a princess.

Even if her father denied his request, she'd stay the course of the dinner next to Duak knowing that he'd tried to make her life just a little bit better.

"Amira," her father said. "Give your seat to Dr. Pettersen."

Leaping over the table would have induced a severe lecture from her mother, so she merely nodded.

Isha leaned close. "Very interesting. We'll speak later about the stranger."

Not if she could help it. She glided around the table because her feet surely weren't touching the marble floor. When she passed Jake in this game of non-musical chairs, he reached out and flittered his finger over the back of her hand. The subtle move weakened her knees to the point that she stumbled. She resumed her stride and made it to Jake's former seat where Calvin stood waiting to assist her to sit. Something Duak hadn't attempted to do.

When the meal and conversation commenced, Calvin looked over at her. "If the king hadn't moved Jake, and the prince had touched you again, I believe the walls would've been redecorated with Prince Duak's blood. I've known him since high school and have never seen him so angry at a complete stranger."

Did he care for her as much as she did him? The fact that he'd spent hours in a plane to finally meet made her lean towards the affirmative. "I'm grateful to him. He saved me from an uncomfortable night."

"And the prince of Ashani from what I suppose is a much needed smack-down."

She glanced up in Jake's direction and couldn't help the smile that came to her lips. Yes, he was extraordinary, and she definitely looked forward to getting to know him even better.

Duak's overblown ego must've thought her smile was directed at him because he winked at her. Once again, her stomach roiled with the upset he caused. Things must be very bad between Bagumi and Ashani if her father had issued an invitation. But she had faith in her father's negotiation skills. He'd settle the issue so that war would be avoided, because no one would win if they fought.

CHAPTER SIX

"What an arrogant ass," Jake mumbled as he strolled through the gardens with Amira at his side. Their escort, this time a security member he hadn't met before, trailed behind them. This must've been how it felt to date in the olden days when a woman's virtue took precedence over privacy.

Amira angled her head up to look at him, and once again, his breath caught. How had he lived so long without her presence alluring him?

"Zareb can be a little cold at times—"

He threw his hands up and waved in denial. "I wasn't talking about him."

No need to have any member of her family thinking him even less worthy of her because he gossiped about them. The fact that they found him so lacking disturbed him. How many times had he been told that he was a catch and that any woman would be lucky to have him? Granted, his mother knew how to stroke his ego, but he'd heard it from other women, too.

Besides, he and his partners had plans to expand their practice. The fact that he had taken the initiative to start his own business in the first place should make him worthier of her than not.

She reached for his arms and brought them down to his sides with a giggle. The warmth of her hands, even through the long sleeves of the dress shirt, eased his trepidation. "I was only joking. I know who you meant. And I wholeheartedly agree. From where I was sitting, it didn't look like you appreciated the conversation you had with him. By the way, thank you for sacrificing yourself."

Amira released him. Would the guard report him to Zareb if he interlinked their fingers? Rather than risk it, he extended an elbow. Without hesitation, she placed her hand in the crook of his arm and stepped closer.

The air no longer felt as humid as it had only a moment before. He tamped down the desire to slip behind one of the tall bushes and nibble her full lips. Would her kisses elicit the same type of excitement in his belly as her touch did?

Clearing his throat, he focused on the present rather than continuing the fantasy of feeling her flesh against his. "I've learned more about the kingdom of Ashani than I know about the history of the United States. By the way, did you realize that Ashani is the greatest territory in all of—" He tapped a finger against his chin pretending to think and then snapped his fingers. "That's right, the world."

Her dark eyes glimmered as her sweet laughter tickled his ears.

"You handled him well, though. At least, you seemed attentive. Much better than I would've done."

What was going on between those two? Duak seemed to want to get friendly with her, but she'd backed away. "From what I know about you, you tend to find the good in everyone. What's wrong with Prince Duak that you can't tolerate being around him?"

For a moment, her body stiffened, and then, she shrugged. "You said it yourself. He's an arrogant man, even for a prince."

The way she looked off into the expansive distance of the property gave him the sense that she hadn't told the truth. What was she hiding?

"Do I need to kick his ass?"

She tipped her head and pursed her lips to the side as if actually considering it. "Can you fight?"

Was she serious? Not willing to release her, he held out his free hand, flexed, and extended it so the scars on his knuckles paled and could be seen even in the moonlight. "In high school and college, I did a bit of kickboxing and won a few tournaments. I keep up with it as a workout. So yes, I can fight."

Gentle fingers grazed the old injuries as she looked up at him. "How come I didn't know that?"

He studied her dark, flawless skin as the tingles skittered down his spine. He refused to ruin the moment by bringing up the fact that she'd never revealed that she was a princess. They'd have that discussion later. "Even if we knew each other for the rest of our lives, it would be impossible to learn everything about each other."

"True."

They walked through an area where a decadent scent wafted through the air. "What kind of flower is that?"

"Jasmine."

He breathed deeply. "It reminds me of you."

Her gentle squeeze of his bicep set off a pleasant quiver in his stomach.

"Nothing gets past you, does it? I have my perfume made from the jasmine we grow in this garden mixed with lemon essence. I find it to be a romantic yet distinctive scent. Not excessively sweet."

"Like you?"

She smacked his arm with her free hand. "Hey. What are you saying?"

He lowered his voice. "I haven't had the chance to taste you yet, but I'm sure you rival the sweetest confection I've ever had."

Rather than pull away at his flirtation, she snuggled closer, pressing the side of her breast against his arm. His groin tightened. How could they get rid of their guard so that he could kiss her? Hell, he was tempted to do so in front of the man, but he respected her too much.

She broke the silence when they reached the edge of the garden and stopped. "Are you still angry with me for not telling you that I'm a princess?"

He sighed and raked his fingers through his hair as he pivoted to face her. "No. I can understand why you didn't. It would've made me feel like less of a fool in front of your brothers if you'd told me, though." He hooked a finger beneath her chin when she lowered her gaze and looked into her eyes. "By now, you should know that it doesn't matter to me. It may have intimidated the hell out of me initially, but I started liking you a long time ago." He looped them around to guide them in the direction of the palace. "It does explain a few things."

Her brows arched. "Such as?"

"Your need to boss me around. Although I do appreciate the texts in the morning telling me what to wear for the day. And my patients really like the ties you guided me into buying."

"I told you."

He laughed. "So you did. I guess this means that if we got married, you'd be laying down royal decrees all the time."

Her feet stilled as her throat bobbed with a hard swallow. "Is that a hypothetical scenario or a realistic one?"

She waved down a hand before he could tell her how much he needed her in his life on more than just a long-distance basis. Was he ready for marriage? With Amira?

Before he'd learned of her princess status, his answer would have readily been yes. But now that he knew, he wondered, like her family, if he had enough to offer her. His dental practice was only just starting to roll out of the red. Even if he reached the peak of what a dentist could make in Middlebury, Vermont, it would never be enough to have her living the high-class lifestyle she'd become accustomed to.

She'd end up despising him if he couldn't provide for her needs. Never had he thought he'd be contemplating that his middle-class status wouldn't be enough for a woman. That he wouldn't be enough for her.

Did he deserve a princess when he held more of a pauper status than not?

"No matter. Forget I asked. Of course it was hypothetical." Her laugh seemed forced, but he accepted the dismissal of the topic.

They walked within their own thoughts through the winding gardens as the multitudes of twinkling stars shone.

He broke the silence a few moments later. "What do you have organized for our vacation here?"

Her teeth gleamed as she smiled. She loved orchestrating events, even his from across the ocean. It was a good thing he didn't mind. Another complementary aspect of their relationship.

"We'll take a proper tour of the palace and its surroundings." Her voice raised in volume as she spoke faster. "You'd be surprised at just how much there is to see here."

He found himself getting as excited as her.

"After that, we'll take it day by day. There are so many beautiful sights in Bagumi that it would wear you out to see them all." She stroked soft fingers down his cheek, leaving a trail of sizzling heat in their wake. He could become addicted to her touch. "I'd like you to get some rest during your visit. You've been working hard at the practice lately and deserve a break."

Damn, he loved this woman. More and more with every moment they spent together. How would he be able to leave her at the end of his vacation? "You're spectacular."

"You're a wise man to recognize it."

He threw his head back and laughed to the night sky. At that moment, no matter how much he lacked according to her family, he could see his life going no other way than with her by his side.

CHAPTER SEVEN

No one could tell Amira that her country wasn't one of the most magnificent in the world. Around the sprawling palace grounds lay a forest with vegetation and animals that wildlife conservatives would salivate over. The waterfall, about five kilometres from the palace and still on their property, had always been a place of solace and ultimate beauty for her.

Knowing that Jake shared her adventurous nature, they'd hiked the distance, listening to the elated songs of the birds on the trek. The sight of antelopes, monkeys, and even a forest elephant during their morning gallivant amazed both Jake and Calvin. The canopy of trees cooled their path, so neither man complained about the weather.

Returning to the palace just before noon, they'd showered, eaten, and driven to a mountainous town about forty kilometres towards the north of Bagumi. The territory displayed panoramic long-distance views that had wowed the men.

As she was accustomed to, security had been with them every step of the way. Although Jake had been focused on the beauty of the land, the sexual tension from last night had swirled around them all day. She'd yearned to explore the unfamiliar sensual force more than she'd wanted to show off the country of her birth.

When was the last time she'd desired a man with such intensity that her palms had itched to touch him? Restricting herself from slipping her hand into his had been a challenge. She represented the throne—jumping on a man in public was not considered acceptable behaviour.

Seated beside Jake in the vehicle on the way back to the palace, he reached for her hand and intertwined their fingers.

"How did you find the day?" Her voice came out a bit breathy.

"Amazing. Bagumi is an incredible country. What you showed me today is so much different from the city we saw when we came from the airport."

"My kingdom is dynamic. You haven't even seen all of it yet." She smiled as she stared into eyes which now reminded her of the ocean when the sun shone brightly during a windy day. A dark turquoise colour. Mysterious and mesmerizing.

Calvin peeked around the back of the passenger's seat. "You're too quiet back there."

Jake clenched his jaw as the driver looked at them through the rear-view mirror.

Sometimes, it grated that the need to be proper stole some of the fun from her life. She attempted to separate their hands. He held on, adding circles against her palm. Her nipples hardened as heat equivalent to the midday sun rushed into her neck and face.

"What do you have planned for us tonight, Princess Amira?" Calvin asked.

She cleared her throat in an attempt to dissipate the arousal Jake was inducing. "After running around all day, I thought you might be too tired to do anything but enjoy a cool shower and then chill at home."

"I can relax when I get back to the States." Calvin waggled his brows. "I'd rather meet new people. Those of the female variety would be best. Especially if they're half as beautiful as you and your sisters. Hell, the queens were hot, too."

The last comment earned him a glower and a click of disapproval from the driver.

Calvin held up both hands and waved them. "No offense, but from what I've seen so far, your women are gorgeous."

"Thank you." Amira answered on behalf of the female contingent of Bagumi. Pride filled her chest as she gloated. "Our women have been represented in Miss World and Miss Universe many times and have won each of them twice."

She paused to let the news sink in before adding the best part about the females of her country. "Most importantly, we're kind-hearted, yet tough." She pointed an index finger at Calvin. "Remember that if you garner the courage to approach one. They won't go easy on you. You must prove to a Bagumian female that you're worthy of her.

Jake angled himself to face her. "And what would it take to do that?"

"Each woman is different. One of my friends once asked a man who fancied her to jump into a lake of crocodile-infested water to prove his manliness."

His head jerked back. "And how did that turn out?"

She giggled. "Once the wound he'd acquired on his calf from one of the more ferocious crocodiles healed, she married him. I have another friend who told the man interested in her to go down into one of our underground gold mining pits."

Calvin raised a brow. "To get her some gold?"

Her dreads flung over her shoulder as she shook her head. "Oh, no. That would be impossible. No one has ever been able to steal Bagumi's gold or diamonds. The security is too tight. My brother Zik ensures it. The man suffered from claustrophobia, and she wanted to test his ability to overcome it. If he could do that, then he could handle anything that came into their lives once they married."

Jake sucked in air through his toothpaste commercial white teeth, making a hissing sound. "Did he?"

"I did," the driver said with a chuckle. "It wasn't until the vows were said that she found out that I passed out as soon as the lift started descending. By that time, she was too hooked to care." He laughed again. "Yes, Bagumian women are demanding, but they're worth every hassle they put you through because they'll always stand by your side."

Jake squeezed her hand. "What about you? What would you make a guy do to prove himself as worthy?"

She leaned against the back of the seat and sighed. "To be honest..." She made sure she had his undivided attention. "Absolutely nothing."

He blinked. "Really?"

"Yes. The man I end up with will possess a power he doesn't need to prove because it's there for the world to see. And me being so wise and observant, I'll know it."

Their gazes held as the air crackled with their attraction. Less than a foot from his tempting lips, she wouldn't move if he leaned down to capture her mouth. Or maybe she'd shift closer. It didn't matter who initiated—all she knew was that she needed his touch.

The car jerked to a stop, snapping her back to reality. Had she been about to kiss him in a car on a public road? Although no one could see them through the tinted windows, it just wasn't done. Especially not by a princess who had two witnesses in the front seat.

Placing her hands over her feverish cheeks did nothing to cool her.

"But if he misbehaves," she said, attempting to clear the air and her mind. "I can have him eat insects to prove his manliness."

That brought a smile to Jake's sexy pink lips. "What kind of challenge is that? I ate some out of curiosity when I was in New Zealand."

"You did not!"

"I was with him." Calvin shivered. "Bleh. I wouldn't touch them."

In her excitement, she placed her hand on his knee. "What did they taste like?"

He covered her fingers. "A bit nutty."

"I see. Well, I think I'll have to think up a less appetizing challenge."

His gaze remained steady on hers. "Anything you ask me to do, Princess, I will."

At that, the last bit of resistance she'd attempted to cultivate against him dissipated.

CHAPTER EIGHT

Amira's idea of a relaxing evening at home after their adventure in the rural areas of Bagumi differed from Jake's. He'd imagined an intimate setting of them getting to know each other while drinking wine. Maybe finally tasting her luscious lips as she sat cradled in his arms.

Her plan consisted of a low-key party with family, a few of her closest friends, a mountain of local foods he couldn't stop eating, and cup upon cup of varying alcoholic beverages served by a private bartender.

The terrace of the massive swimming pool served as the backdrop for the gathering. The instrumental live band's music set the tone for the evening. Chill. Just as she'd promised.

Calvin's laughter could be heard from the other side of the pool. His friend was having the time of his life with the attention he'd garnered from the females of the group.

For some reason, most likely Amira's possessive hand on Jake's arm when a woman came close to him, they steered clear of him. He didn't mind one bit. She'd captured his heart, and he had eyes for no one else.

Once they'd returned to the palace after their outing, she'd left his side for a few hours. He'd missed her as if he wouldn't see her again for the next year.

And now, he watched her engage with everyone at the party, ensuring their comfort. How many times had she made the group she'd been conversing with laugh? Too many to count. She gave her whole presence to a person when she communicated, leaving no doubt of where her focus lay.

He'd been happy to learn about the equality of the sexes in Bagumi. They didn't raise their females to be timid. He wouldn't know how to deal with someone who always agreed with him instead of stating her true opinion. He'd gone out with such women in the past, and their relationships hadn't gone beyond the first date.

A movement to his right caught his attention. Duak stepped through the terrace's glass doors with a snarl of distaste and joined the party. Jake stood on the balls of his feet, ready to pounce. He watched as the other man scanned the area. His expression changed as he set his eyes on Amira. His narrowed gaze and slick grin could only be interpreted as greed.

Jake sauntered to Amira's side, reaching her before Duak. He blocked the other man's view of her with his back, leaned close, and whispered in her ear. "If you don't dim down your beauty, the stars will get jealous."

The corny line had just the effect he'd intended as she slapped his shoulder and laughed. "Good one."

"Princess Amira." She snapped her shoulders back at the sharp tone coming from their left. "Is it your mother who taught you such a deplorable way of behaving? Such a lack of propriety." Duak stepped closer to where Jake held his hand at her lower back. "How dare you allow a man who is not your husband to touch you in such a manner?"

Just as Jake was about to face off with the rude monarch, Amira stepped between them.

"How dare *you*?" Her voice was low, yet powerful. "You have insulted both me and the first queen of Bagumi in the same breath while on our land.

For an even lesser insurrection, I could have you punished. Prince or not."

Jake didn't know if she really could, but he wanted to cheer at the way she'd pronounced the declaration. Yes, his woman certainly owned her royalness.

"Do not think," she continued, "that you can speak to me in such a manner ever again. I am a grown woman, not some child you can bully around. History will not repeat itself."

Not even knowing what their past held, Jake's face flushed with anger, and his fists clenched, ready to punch the man, but Amira maintained her position, standing in his way. He took a moment to calm down. He was normally level-headed in all situations, but the thought of Amira being terrorized brought out the rage in him.

The prince's gaze stroked her from head to toe. "You certainly are a woman. *My* woman."

She crossed both arms over her chest and flexed her fingers against her bare upper arms, indenting the skin. Jake had a feeling she wanted to do some fighting of her own.

"I'm my own person. I told you two years ago that I would never marry you. Nothing has or will ever change."

Jake glanced down at her while trying to keep his lips sealed, then back up at Duak.

The bastard was grinning.

"There's nothing I desire that I do not receive, my princess." He narrowed his gaze at Jake. "Do not touch her again."

Jake weaved around Amira and dove towards him only to be restrained by a strong arm against his chest as Duak scampered backward. Knowing that

Amira's small frame couldn't hold him back, a look to the right met Zareb's eyes. Was the man everywhere?

The head of security released him as he spoke. "So far, I know you to be an intelligent man."

The words of admonishment sank in, and Jake rolled his shoulders back with a nod.

Amira's nostrils flared. "You should've let Jake beat the arrogance out of him."

Zareb chuckled. "Maybe next time when we aren't on Bagumi soil. At the palace, no less."

Jake looked around. The scene hadn't drawn anyone else's attention as Calvin still entertained his groupies. His gaze returned to Duak who, for a dark-skinned man, looked a lot paler than before.

Duak pointed to Amira and Zareb. "You both bore witness. The barbarian attempted to attack me."

Zareb shook his head with a frown.

"I heard most of the conversation, Duak. If you had spoken to me the way you had our guest, I would not be held accountable for my actions." He sent a glance in the direction of his sister. "Why didn't you tell me he used to bully you? I would've taken care of him." He rotated his head to glower at the now hunch-shouldered prince. "In fact, I still may."

Duak's whimper didn't go unnoticed. "We were children. Time has passed, and we have matured."

Jake wasn't sure if Amira smiled at her overprotective brother's open threat or Duak's trembling voice.

"Yes," she said as she tangled her arm through Jake's. "I have matured."

With Amira having the last word, she led Jake to the other side of the pool with a broad-as-the-moon smile on her face. As if an argument hadn't just broken out, she proceeded to engage with a few of her friends, making sure to include him in the conversation.

His heart swelled. Put the woman in any situation, and she would excel. It didn't hurt that she was beautiful, intelligent, and kind beyond measure, either. She was the woman he'd been searching for all of his life. Letting her go was no longer an option.

His Defiant Princess

CHAPTER NINE

It had been impossible to push the ugly scene with Duak out of her mind as the evening had progressed. Although Jake's presence had eased the tension coiled in her belly, she couldn't stop the occasional shiver of dread as she thought about Duak's smug and all-knowing sneer when he'd called her his woman.

"Are you okay?" Jake asked as he slid a hand along her lower back, oozing electric shocks into her skin.

Zareb only missed the move because he was busy trying to keep a drunk Calvin from touching the priceless artwork that her father would surely have him empty his bank account and serve at the palace for if he destroyed it. Other than his family and ruling the kingdom, there was very little the king enjoyed more than the rare pieces of art he collected from all over the world.

"I'm cool," she answered. "Did you enjoy the party?"

He slowed their pace. "Do you know that whenever you use the word cool, I know you aren't. Now tell me what's going on."

She glanced up at him. Did he really want to know, or was he being polite? The earnestness in his eyes gave her the answer. She would've shared with him if they were still communicating electronically, anyway. She'd come to rely on his listening ear and opinions.

"I'm worried about what Duak said."

Aside from the clenching of his jaw, he didn't respond. Just waited for her to continue.

"He normally makes my skin crawl, but what he said and how he called me *his* with such confidence went beyond creepy."

When he propped an arm around her shoulders, she leaned against him, soaking in his strength. Something she hadn't been able to do with a man outside of her family. She'd never known someone not blood related that she could trust to support her. Even though they'd never met, during the time they'd known each other, he'd always been there for her. And now, with him physically at her side, she appreciated him even more.

"He was just talking," Jake said. "First and foremost, you're your own woman. No one can claim you unless you allow it. And you certainly didn't give yourself to him."

"Never. When I was eight and he eleven, his family came to visit. We played hide and seek in the forest behind the palace. When I found him in less than two minutes, he grabbed my arm and dragged me to the edge of a ravine. He told me that I had cheated and must be taught a lesson. And then, he pushed me."

Jake jerked back. "Down the ravine?"

"Yes. Lucky for me, it wasn't steep. Except for a few scrapes and bruises, I didn't get hurt."

Zareb turned with his features tight. "I would have killed him. I still might."

Jake released his hold on her. She wanted it back.

"And that's why I didn't tell any of you. You've eased up on your overprotective tendencies over the years, but back then, I feared for his life. I told Mama that I had fallen."

"Did he do anything else to you?" Jake spoke before Zareb could, his face a replica of the flared nostrils and bulging jawed expression of wrath as her brother's.

The scoundrel had stolen her first kiss and had attempted to gain more from her when she'd been sixteen. Using the self-defence manoeuvres that her karate instructor had taught her, she'd gotten out of Duak's hold before he could do more than leave her with a pounding heart and weak knees as she ran away. She'd looked back only once to find him rolling on the ground clutching his groin.

Unsure of how people would view her, she'd never told anyone about what he'd done. Regret had followed her that her first kiss hadn't been freely given.

It had taken time, and she'd spoken about it with her best friend, but then, she'd buried the incident so that it no longer interfered with her dealings with non-familial men. Telling Jake and Zareb about the incident would only lead to bloodshed.

"Before then, he would taunt me, but after that, I stayed away from him whenever he came to visit." *Except for the one time he tricked me into getting me alone.* "There's no need to go after him."

"Like hell," Zareb said at the same time Jake growled.

What had she started? Her heart melted to think that Jake cared about her as much as she did him. And then, a moment of doubt hit her. Did he care, or was it just his nature to be protective of his friends?

Brushing her uncharacteristic uncertainty aside, she focused on Zareb's potential retaliation on Duak and rushed to his side. When had he slung Calvin onto his shoulder? She ignored it for the moment. "Promise me you won't do or say anything to him. Bagumi is having enough issues with his country as it stands.

You doing something undiplomatic would start a war. Our people don't need death and destruction. Peace is always better. Isn't that what you always preach?"

Zareb grunted. "If he ever lays a hand on you again—"

"I'll tear him apart," Jake completed.

She blinked, unbelieving at the smile her brother gave the man she loved. Would wonders never cease? All it took was Jake being as overprotective of her as her family to get into Zareb's good graces. Now, she'd need to have a chat with Jake about how she could take care of herself.

But first, she'd wipe away her own grin and try to dim down her glow of pride as they completed the walk to Jake's suite.

Inside, Zareb settled Calvin on the couch.

"No more alcohol for your friend while he's here." He headed towards the still-open door. "Jake, have a good night. Amira, I expect you to be in your room in fifteen minutes."

He swaggered out, leaving both of them open-mouthed that he'd left them alone.

"I think you made an impression on him with your macho declaration of violence earlier."

Jake and Amira jumped at Calvin's voice.

Calvin got to his feet and rubbed his abdomen. "The man is a machine. He carried me without losing his breath. As if I weighed no more than a five-year-old. I wouldn't want to be his enemy." He shook his head and walked towards his room with a suspiciously steady gait. "It's a good thing I'm able to resist the temptation of alcohol, isn't it? That ban would've put a damper on my holiday," he said with a wink. "Have a good night, you two."

They watched as he closed the panel behind him, then burst into laughter at the same time.

"Your friend is a handful," she said.

"I know."

When silence filled the room, awareness settled around them. For the first time ever, they were alone together.

He took a step towards her. "How long does it take to get to your room from here?"

The space between them closed further as she made her own move in his direction. "It's at the opposite end of the palace, so about five minutes at a brisk pace. If I sprint, I'll get there in two and a half."

A foot separated them. Who would make the first move and bring them to the point where their attraction had been driving them for the past two days? No, one year.

His gaze lowered to her mouth before returning to her eyes. "Princess Amira, may I have permission to kiss you?"

Anticipation had her heart thudding hard. "Yes."

Jake cleared the space and framed her face with his hands. She savoured the moment of closeness by closing her eyes as he took his time to descend his head towards hers. Their lips met in a final rush as time stood still. Her mouth opened under his, allowing for his cognac-infused tongue to meld with hers to the point of dizziness.

She gripped at his back as she revelled in his exploration of her mouth and body. Her experiences with the opposite sex had been negligible. Yet, never had she thought kissing him would feel so right that she couldn't imagine being anywhere else. Love flowed into every caress of her lips, every stroke of her tongue. Jake was all she knew. She'd never desire anyone else.

A sharp knock sounded. Their heads sprang apart as their arms clung to each other while they stared in amazement, attempting to catch their breath. Dark sapphires looked back at her, and she stood on her toes for more of what they'd just shared.

Banging had them springing apart before she realized it had come from inside the suite, not outside.

Jake gave a lopsided grin. "I think Calvin's acting as our alarm clock."

Still trying to catch her breath, she whispered, "I don't want to go."

He rested his forehead against hers. "I don't want you to, either."

They stayed in that position until Calvin finally came out.

"Your tank of a brother was being kind. Don't take advantage of it."

And then, he slipped back into his room, leaving them to do the right thing.

Peeling apart, they held hands as they strolled to the door.

"I'll walk you back," Jake offered.

She wanted nothing more, but shook her head. For once, she'd follow the rules, hoping she'd get rewarded for it. "I'll see you tomorrow."

Why did she find it so hard to leave him? What would she do when he disappeared from her home? The thought hurt, and she wasn't sure she'd be able to survive his leaving if this overnight parting was turning out to be so difficult.

Kissing first his left then right cheek, she stroked her hand down his arm to his fingertips as she backed away. "Have a good night."

"You, too."

She turned and walked down the never-ending hallway, feeling the heat of his gaze until she turned the corner. Her phone buzzed, indicating a message. It was from Zareb.

"You've done well, my sister."

The man wasn't head of security for nothing.

One question still haunted her. What would she do when Jake went back to the US? How would she cope?

She'd never thought of leaving Bagumi. The only home she'd ever known. Everyone she'd ever loved was there. When she'd gone to Switzerland for her masters, she'd been incredibly lonely. In hindsight, that was a good thing because it had allowed her to meet Jake in a way to make a new friend, even if he had been thousands of miles away.

That one year away had convinced her that home was the best place for her. She doubted she could ever live anywhere else than the place of her birth.

And then, Jake's piercing gaze came to mind. When she was with him, she knew she belonged at his side, but was she willing to leave the security and love of her family for something that only held the potential of greatness?

With everything that had happened that day, Jake should've been asleep moments after hanging up with Amira. They'd spoken for a couple of hours once she'd returned to her room. The racing of his thoughts wouldn't let him rest. Figuring that jet-lag also played a role, he gave up the attempt and went into the living area of the suite only to find Calvin seated on the couch watching television.

"What are you doing up?" he asked as he went to the kitchenette, reached into the mini-fridge, and pulled out a bottle of water.

"I could ask you the same question, but I already know the answer."

Jake sat on the armchair and rested his elbows on his knees. The unopened bottle dangled between his fingers. "I'm hooked."

"You, my friend, are caught, scaled, gutted, and filleted. You were even before arriving here."

He couldn't deny it. Conversations with Amira had been amazing. He'd never gotten to know someone so completely before. Yes, she was a stunning woman, but with the time they'd invested in talking, he'd learned so much about her.

The tentative sweetness of her kisses had melted his insides. And then, she'd given herself over to him, and things had gone wild. He should've known they'd be explosive together.

Incredible.

"So what are you going to do about it?"

The question snapped him out of the memory of Amira's pliant lips against his. He opened the water and drank until his throat felt less parched. "About what?"

"Your relationship."

It was the question that had kept him awake for the past hour. "Marry her."

"Of course you will. You'd be an idiot to let her go, especially after finding out just how much chemistry you two have." Calvin relaxed into the couch and rested an ankle across his knee. "Where will you live?"

Not the question he'd expected, but one which plagued him.

"I don't know." He scraped a hand through his hair. "Before we arrived in Bagumi, I knew for certain that if we got along in person, then she'd come back to Vermont with me."

"Even knowing her dream of working for her family in a larger capacity?"

When Calvin put it that way, he sounded like a jerk for not acknowledging her career. Or her family ties, for that matter. Had he thought about her needs at all when he'd presumed she'd pick up her things and move across the sea with him?

And now that he'd experienced her world, he questioned if she'd be willing to leave. She lived like the proverbial princess in a home she loved surrounded by family and a whole country who adored her. Would she leave it all for love? For him?

His heart spasmed. What if she didn't love him? The though had never crossed his mind. He'd presumed she felt the same.

But then, he relaxed as memories assaulted him. The way she'd looked at him, clung to him, and attempted to break the rules to be together told him everything he needed to know. If she didn't feel the same way now, she would soon, especially once he proved to her just how worthy he was to have her in his life. He may not have money or prestige, but he'd do anything to make her happy. Anything. He shivered hoping he wouldn't have to let a snake wind itself around him to prove it.

"We'll work it out," he stated, his confidence returning.

Calvin studied him. "Are you ready to tell me what the queen said to you when Zareb dragged you out of here the day we arrived?" He rubbed his chin and smirked. "I still can't believe we're hanging around with actual royalty."

He'd been sworn to secrecy from saying anything to Amira, but did it mean he couldn't confide in Calvin? A shiver of dread skidded down his back at the memory of the audience with the powerful woman. While the princes had attempted to intimidate him with their posturing and harsh words of warning, it hadn't had even half the effect that they'd presumed. He also knew how to intimidate when he needed to.

As soon as Amira's mother had looked at him, his knees had weakened, and it had taken a concerted effort of straightening his legs for him not to humiliate himself by tumbling to the floor. He'd kept his back straight and bowed at the waist just like he'd seen on television. He'd wished he'd paid more attention to how people treated the royalty in England, but who knew he'd ever be faced with any himself.

"You saw her at dinner, she's amazing. Amira resembles her in so many ways that I can see her at the same age."

"Lucky you, man."

Jake chuckled. "I know. If I end up looking anything like my dad, people are going to wonder how much money I possess to rob the cradle even though we're nearly the same age."

"What did she say to you to make you look all wild-eyed when you returned?"

"It wasn't exactly what she said, but how she said it."

Calvin laughed. "Dude, you sound like a woman."

"If you don't want to hear what happened, then keep up the insults."

"Fine." His chuckle died out with a sigh. "No more honest observations."

Doubtful. "She possesses a...an authority that I can't describe. I've never experienced anything like it before. It was as if my will had disappeared and I was ready to do anything she said. Like being with my own mother, but only a hundred times greater."

He'd expected to be nervous when he'd met her, not charmed.

Calvin slid to the edge of the couch. "So what did she say?"

"She asked me questions about how Amira and I met."

"Did you tell her? The brothers warned you."

Not one bit ashamed, Jake nodded. "Didn't you hear what I just said? She's way more powerful than her children combined. I told her everything! I mean everything. Who I had dated in the past. My plans for my career. How I feel about Amira. My intentions toward her. Everything."

"Whoa," Calvin breathed the word out as if he hadn't left high school years ago.

"I know. And then, she asked me a question that had every inch of my skin looking like a damn lobster."

"What?"

Jake stood and stretched wide as he yawned. "I can't tell you. Something about 'off with my head' if I mentioned it to anyone. I'm going to bed. Amira's taking us to the capital tomorrow."

Calvin got to his feet. "You're just going to leave me on the ledge like that and not tell me?"

"Yes. Have a good night."

He left his friend feeling more relieved about his relationship with Amira. Not one hundred percent assured, but closer to it than he'd been.

Nana Prah

CHAPTER TEN

The morning they'd spent together had been glorious. Even though Amira hadn't gotten the chance to be alone with Jake again, she'd enjoyed their trip into Darusa. The nation's capital was a modern city of skyscrapers, endless shops, and restaurants which provided authentic food from countries all over the world.

"I'm going to sit at the bar and have a drink," Calvin said with a conspiratorial wink after they'd eaten lunch at her favourite Ethiopian restaurant. "Non-alcoholic, of course."

Amira's face heated at the memory of last night. "The man isn't subtle at all."

"Never has been. But his heart is as big as the Grand Canyon. And I won't get started on his business acumen. He's a genius." Jake leaned toward her. "Don't tell him I told you, but he's the one keeping our practice afloat."

"So dentists aren't prolific business men?"

He chuckled. "Not the ones who work with me. We're close to finalizing the plans he came up with of opening another office in a couple of years."

He'd mentioned the venture before but had never sounded as sure about it actually happening. She clapped as his enthusiasm for his future made her giddy. "That's wonderful."

"We all think so."

She stared into his sparkling blue eyes, not believing that they were alone together. Of course, the restaurant was filled so she couldn't crawl into his lap and continue the amazing kisses from last night.

Unable to hold hands because it would garner stares, just being with him thrilled her.

"I missed you last night."

His smooth, sexy voice caressed her.

She licked her lips recalling how they'd tingled under his. "I missed you, too."

Never in her life had she felt the need to be with a man every waking moment.

He reached out to touch her hand resting on the table, and then must've thought better of it when it landed beside hers. "How about if we ditch the bodyguard and go somewhere we can be alone?"

She angled her head, unable to keep the frown from her face. "I wish we could, but I fear Zareb's retaliation."

His upper body shook as if shivering, and she giggled.

"Seriously, there must be a way we can spend time by ourselves."

She nodded. "I'm working on it. My mother has been on me about finding someone to get into a relationship with. Once I tell her I'm in lo—" She slammed her lips together, incredulous at what she'd been about to reveal.

Jake leaned over the table, bringing him closer. "What were you about to say?"

How could she have let the words slip out so easily? What if he didn't feel the same? She shook her head. "Nothing."

"Sweetheart, would it help if I told you I love you? I've been in love with you for months."

All her life, she'd been given everything her heart desired. She'd never appreciated anything more than hearing his words of affection because she'd yearned for them for so long. As if all of her dreams had come

72

true in one fell swoop because she loved him so much in return. Yet, she her greedy ears need more confirmation.

She brought a hand to her chest. "Really?"

"Without a doubt. A day doesn't go by without me thinking about you at least a thousand times. You consume my world, Amira."

What had she done to deserve this amazing man sitting in front of her instead of communicating on her phone screen? "I love you, too, Jake."

Rather than scrambling over the table and falling into his arms like she was propelled to do, they sat staring and smiling into each other's eyes. Every organ in her body morphed into something gooey, and she swore she'd end up a puddle on the floor.

Her phone vibrated before her father's special ringtone of drumming hit her ears. She wrenched her gaze from Jake's to look down at her cell and frowned. Her father rarely called her while she was in Bagumi. "I have to take this."

When she clicked the answer button, her gut twisted into painful knots. "Good afternoon, Baba."

"Good afternoon, Amira. How is the excursion with your guests?"

She flung her gaze up to Jake's and gave him a reassuring smile at his concerned grimace. "It's going well. They're impressed with how modern Darusa is."

"As well they should be." The pride in his voice couldn't be missed. "I'd like you to come home. I have some news to share with you."

She raised her brows. It would be useless to ask him to tell her over the phone, but it must be important to warrant a call from him instead of ordering Zawadi to inform her.

"We'll leave right now."

"Good." His voice sounded as stern as it always did when he made a call. "I expect you in my office in two hours. Wear the family cloth."

Something official enough to warrant her to wear the official Royal House of Saene print cloth couldn't be bad. Could it?

Even if it was, it probably didn't involve her. After all, she was his favourite child. The light of his eye. At least, that's what she liked to believe. Maybe he wanted to show her off to some special guests who had arrived. "Yes, Baba. I'll see you soon."

She reached for her purse and placed the phone inside as she tried to hide her unfounded trepidation of the upcoming meeting and disappointment at having to end the day with Jake. "We have to go. My father wants to see me."

"Is everything okay?" he asked as he stood.

"I wouldn't be so nervous if Zawadi had called with the same message."

Jake tapped Calvin on the shoulder as they passed him. "Let's go."

They walked to the car with their escort.

She was usually good at keeping herself optimistic, but for some reason, a niggling doubt she couldn't rationalize refused to leave her. Random possibilities of what could be wrong at the palace played through her mind. Maybe Duak had spun a ridiculous tale about what had happened last night, and her father was displeased. Perhaps her father had discovered that she'd been alone with Jake and wanted to send him away.

She inhaled in an attempt to calm her nerves. None of the options would warrant her having to change her clothes.

"What's it like to have a king as a father?"

The question wasn't new to her, but it was the first time Jake had shown interest in her royal status. "I could say its glorious and glamorous, which it is sometimes because I get treated like...well, a princess, and I love it. But other times, it's annoying because of the restrictions."

Distracted by the topic, she angled her body towards him in the back seat. "Have you ever read the book or seen the movie the *Prince and the Pauper*?"

He nodded. "By Mark Twain. We had to read it in the sixth grade. I couldn't figure out why the prince would ever want to leave the palace, even if it was unintentional."

"Me, neither." She waggled a finger. "A world without privilege is not a place for me."

Jake's face blanched.

She held back a grimace at having bragged to the man who'd just professed his love, but who had never lived a life anywhere close to the extravagance delivered to her on a daily basis. She couldn't draw the words back because she'd meant them.

Damage control. "I'm not saying that I *couldn't* live a simpler life, though."

Not as effective as she'd intended. Weak, really.

"Are you okay?"

"Yes." He tugged at the collar of his shirt. "I'm still waiting for the air conditioner to completely kick in."

She didn't blame him for lying. How would they rectify the contrast in their statures? Did love conquer everything, including financial differences? She looked into his eyes and knew she'd always love him, money or not. He was a good man and treated her well. What more could she ask for?

He cleared his throat. "Go on with the story."

"Well, my point about the book was that every day is not tiaras and roses. You'd think I could lie about all day and be fed my favourite foods while undergoing spa treatments."

Her vision glazed over at the potential of such a life. And then, she remembered what it had actually been like to grow up as the daughter of the king.

"Not at all," she continued. "We had to excel at academics because no child of my parents would give less than their best. And then, there were the activities."

She plopped against the seat, exhausted from just thinking about them.

"Like what?" Jake snuck his hand across the space between them and touched her fingers, letting them linger.

The zip of current revived her.

"You name it. Dance, which included ballet, tap, and jazz. Sports of all kinds, including gymnastics, fencing, martial arts, football." Remembering his culture, she added, "The real kind where you can only kick the ball, not the American type."

He grinned. "You mean soccer."

She arched a brow. The royal equivalent of rolling her eyes. "I mean football. Field hockey, tennis, swimming, and so many others. And then, I had to take specialty lessons like etiquette, sewing, piano, flute, and violin." She stopped to take a dramatic breath. "Debate, acting, French, Spanish, art, conversations for the worldly, coo—"

He held up a hand. "You had me up until conversations for the worldly. What's that?"

"The bane of my existence." Her comment set him laughing. "According to the many lectures my mother has given me about being a royal, we are

76

considered to be diplomats and should represent our kingdom well. This means we need to be able to converse with anyone at any time about anything."

He scrunched his brows. "Is that possible?"

She grinned. "Ask me a question. Something you think I have absolutely no knowledge about."

He tapped his chin as he thought for a moment. "Back in college, I suffered through *Eugene Onegin* by Alexander Pushkin. Have you ever read it?"

"Unfortunately, no. The only Russian novel I've ever read was *The Funeral Party* by Lyudmila Ulitskaya. A complex and remarkable book." She gave him the slightest of smiles. "Being a great thinker yourself, I'm sure you'd enjoy it."

His chest puffed out as he smiled. And then, he cocked his head as realization seemed to dawn. "Hey."

She giggled.

"You didn't actually talk about the book."

"But—" she held up a finger, "—from his name I know the author is Russian, proceeded to relate it to something I did know, and then complimented you. That's what conversation for the worldly is all about. Getting you to feel good about having spoken to me. I'm pretty good at it. I've impressed my tutor on many occasions."

His eyes glittered. "I can imagine you're good at a lot of things. So being a princess is hard work?"

"No. All you have to do is be born into a royal house." She swiped her dreads behind her ear. "Becoming a good, well-rounded princess is."

"Tell me, Princess Amira," he said in a lowered voice after leaning closer. "Did you charm me into falling in love with you, or was it purely destiny?"

Her breath caught in pleasure at his words.

"I'd say both," she said in a returned whisper. "As you have learned and come to appreciate, I am an extraordinary woman with exquisite taste."

"And ever so humble." He took a risk and pressed his lips against hers.

Her heart soared as she accepted his kiss without falling into it like she wanted to. If only they were alone, she'd taste the deliciousness of his mouth until she were satisfied.

She blinked and held herself back from grasping his shirt and drawing him to her. "I try."

Once again, his laughter filled the car. He continued to distract her with conversation for the rest of the ride home, this time adding Calvin into the mix.

As they walked through the palace doors, he asked, "Do you want me to come with you?"

She wished he could. She found so much reassurance and strength from his presence that she felt invincible when with him. "My father called for only me. It would be rude to bring an uninvited guest before the king."

He raised a hand towards her. She shuffled in an attempt to avoid his touch. Respecting her position was paramount, especially with people roaming the corridors undertaking their duties. She ignored the guilt she felt at the slight slump of his shoulders.

"I have to change before I meet my father."

He nodded. "Call me and let me know what happened."

"I will."

She backed away one step, then a second, before waving and turning to head towards her room. She discovered Jake watching her when she glanced over her shoulder. She gave him a curved hand beauty queen wave with her widest smile. How could life get any better?

Differences aside, there was no doubt that they belonged together, and one day, they would.

CHAPTER ELEVEN

Amira's gold heels clicked double time on her way to her father's office. Dressed in a modest ankle-length mermaid skirt with its matching three-quarter-sleeved top, the rich purple, hand-woven cloth had the gold Royal House of Saene seal embossed into it. Only members of the royal house were allowed to wear it.

Not finding her father's secretary present, she knocked and avoided switching from foot to foot as she waited for permission to enter.

Holding her head so that if her mother appeared and planted a book on it, the tome would stay in place, she glided into the room when someone opened the door.

At least twenty people filled the large office. She covered her surprise by bowing her head. She placed her hands on her upper thighs and bent at the hips to her father before assessing the room. The King of Ashani sat to her left. She bowed the same way to him while attempting to ignore Duak at his father's right hand. His entourage of frowning men didn't induce a sense of respect within her. For as long as she'd known them, the people of Ashani had been allergic to anything resembling a genuine smile.

The last demonstration of deference fell to her mother, her stepmother, and the five queens from the Ashani kingdom who were seated at the opposite side of the room flanked by Zawadi and Zareb whose expressionless faces didn't give her a clue about what was going on. Her mother smiled at her and nodded. The rest of the people on her familial side of the room consisted of palace guards.

What was going on? Rather than ask, she stood as still as a statue until her father spoke. If things were any more formal, she'd expect a linguist to speak for him, but she hadn't see any of the people who often took on the role of talking on the King's behalf.

"You are welcome, my daughter." Her father indicated to the chair at his right hand side—the position usually reserved for her mother as the first wife and queen mother of Bagumi. "Sit."

Without hesitation, but becoming more confused by the moment, she took her place.

Goose bumps formed along her arms as a chill ran down her spine. She stifled the shiver, not wanting to draw any more critical attention to herself than every eye in the room was already giving her.

As was his manner, her father took ages before speaking again. How could anyone question where she received her penchant for drama?

"Today is a most auspicious day," he said in English for the benefit of their guests. Although their lands bordered, they'd never shared a local language. "A day to mark in the history books as one of true accomplishment." He held up a sheaf of papers. "An official arrangement has been made between the Kingdom of Bagumi and the Kingdom of Ashani regarding the river bordering our lands. It is a significant day indeed because no blood was shed in reaching the agreement. Once again, peace prevails between the kingdoms."

Everyone in the room clapped. Avoiding the loss of lives was a coup for both countries. Amira celebrated with the others, happy that the situation had ended without conflict. It didn't bode well that her stomach still quivered with nervousness.

Her father waved, and the applause subsided.

"King Lahib has requested that we seal the peace between our lands with a marriage."

Her hands trembled as the dread built. She attempted to control it with rationalization as her father's speech about the history of the two countries droned on. Maybe one of her siblings had fallen in love with someone from the Ashani kingdom and had decided to marry? None of them had mentioned dating anyone recently, but they didn't share everything they did. After all, she hadn't told them about Jake.

As much as she attempted to convince herself otherwise, her head tingled with alarm as reality started sinking in, pushing out the last of her optimism.

This wasn't supposed to happen. Not when she'd grown up believing she'd be able to marry a man of her choosing. A man she'd fallen in love with.

A lifetime of bondage to someone in this day and age was supposed to be voluntary. Time had been on her side for getting to know the man she'd spend the rest of her life with. No one had pressured her to find someone to marry. After all, her older sisters were still single. She'd held no delusions that they'd get married in any kind of order, but neither had the possibility occurred that she'd be forced to marry, either.

Jake.

She gripped her trembling hands together at the terror of losing him.

Her journey of growth and experience had led her right to him. She'd found the love of her life. The man who made her heart swell just by talking to him. Now that they were together, she knew for certain that they were meant to be together. He hadn't asked her to marry him, but first came love and then came...

She forced herself to listen to the rest of her father's diatribe. Maybe she was overreacting.

"Prince Duak Omiata, the first born male of King Lahib, has requested the hand of my youngest daughter, Princess Amira Oware Saene, for marriage."

A sharp gasp pierced Amira's ears, and it took her a moment to realize she'd been the one to emit it. *No, no, no.* It couldn't be true.

She glanced at her family, and her skin went cold at the smiles and applause she witnessed. The deplorable realization that her father would give her away as a prize for the prince of arrogant fools brought on a sharp pain at her temples.

Accepting the decision would mean defying what she'd known all of her life. That she mattered to her father as more than a political pawn. That her happiness and wellbeing meant absolutely nothing to him.

The room came back into focus even though her breathing remained shallow and her heart rate erratic. She looked at her brothers, and for a moment, their widened eyes showed as much surprise as they were capable of in public. At least, they hadn't known and failed to tell her. The betrayal would've cut too deep.

Her mother smiled and nodded as she accepted accolades from the others.

Queen Zulekha, the first wife of the king, had married him through an arranged marriage. And now, her daughter would to marry in the same manner. She'd see it as a great honour. A boon to her already elevated stature within the kingdom. Not only would her daughter be the first to marry in the family, but she'd seal the bond between two countries.

Amira's shock transitioned in a flash as the room shimmered with a red haze. The pain in her jaws barely registered as she grit her teeth and balled her fists, wanting to plant them in the gut of the person responsible for her involvement in the situation. Duak!

He'd attempted to claim her, but she'd refused. His pride had led him to manipulate the situation. She'd credit him with plotting the whole thing, including the border squirmishes, if he wasn't so short-sighted. He'd merely taken advantage when the opportunity had presented itself.

How dare they attempt to control her? She was no longer a child. They'd raised her to be independent and self-determined, yet, in one statement, her father had disintegrated everything she'd ever known about her place in the world. He hadn't even had enough respect for her to confer with her about it first.

At that moment, she knew one thing to be absolutely true; she wouldn't marry Duak. Her heart had already been claimed by Jake. For the first time in her life, she'd found love, and she refused to give it up for an arrogant, self-centred, controlling shadow of a man.

Not even the love for her country and her people would permit her to sacrifice her life and well-being. Not even the threat of war between the two kingdoms would make her marry that tyrant. She'd rather take up arms herself and fight the Ashani.

At the fierceness of the thought which would never come to fruition, Amira shifted pleading eyes to her brothers. Zareb's jaw looked so tight that he might crack a tooth any moment. Zawadi's expression remained neutral. He waved a hand in her direction, indicating that she should keep calm and wait.

Staying quiet was the last thing she wanted to do as blood pounded in her ears. The rage pulsing through her, driving her to shout like a woman who'd been betrayed by those who meant most to her, was too strong to restrain.

Just as her feet rocked to propel her up, she held herself bound to the seat through sheer will, refraining from destroying her family's reputation by behaving in a manner beneath their expectations. No matter how much she wanted to claw her nails into Duak's eyes and hear the high-pitched scream she'd induced years ago with a kick to his groin, she resisted.

She controlled her breathing with deep inhales so that passing out from lack of oxygen was no longer an issue even as she still seethed. Counting backward from five as she envisioned puppies frolicking beneath a rainbow allowed her tight muscles to slacken a little more.

Her father raised both hands to quiet the raucous jubilation. When everyone fell silent, he continued. "The marriage ceremony will occur in one month."

She sat back as the new information penetrated. A month wasn't as long as she would've liked, but she'd be able to develop a plan to somehow have her father reverse the decision of trading her off to the Kingdom of Ashani. A month would be enough time to help him realize what a horrible mistake it would be to marry her off to the idiot. The optimism that had crept into her helped her believe that, in the end, they would call off the wedding to ensure her happiness.

After all, her father loved her. He just needed to be guided in a different direction to ensure peace between their countries. Believing otherwise would lead her to a mental breakdown.

Her potential chance at a reprieve didn't last as her father made yet another proclamation.

"As a sign of good faith, as suggested by King Lahib, Amira will travel in three days' time to live in Ashani until one week before the wedding."

Whispers of incredulity amongst her side of the room broke out at the non-traditional announcement. Her mother's brows furrowed and her lips pursed at the news.

Her father's betrayal had compounded with each announcement. Gone was the calm she'd striven so hard for over the interminably long gathering.

The hurricane of emotions from the past few minutes brought on a state of fatigue like she'd never known. She gripped the sides of her chair to keep from falling. Her body shook, and sweat slid down her face despite the air conditioning as terror alone remained.

The surety of being able to control her destiny that she'd been convinced of a few seconds ago had slipped through her grasp, leaving her with nothing. Hope no longer remained as she blinked back the burn in her eyes.

She sniffed and swallowed hard because she'd been taught to always represent the crown as strong. Tears were seen as weak, and she shouldn't indulge. Not until she was alone. She doubted she'd be able to wait much longer and her pain would be laid bare to everyone gathered.

A glance at her straight-backed mother whose smile had completely vanished, replaced by an unreadable mask, stared at her. The slight lift of the queen's chin reinforced that her breakdown had to wait. She sucked in air and held it until her lungs ached for release. When forced by her body to exhale, the lump in her throat no longer threatened to choke her.

Giving up on having the life she wanted, one of love and true companionship, wasn't an option. She'd been taught to strive for the best because she was worthy of anything she desired.

Jake's earnest eyes as he'd told her he loved her flashed into her mind. She'd fight her father's decision. She had too much to lose if she didn't.

CHAPTER TWELVE

Jake sensed a change in the energy of the palace as he and Calvin walked along the marbled hallways. The air held a tinge of excitement as people smiled and gesticulated wildly with their hands as they spoke.

They entered the dining room to be met by what seemed to be a party rather than a dinner. None of the reserved quiet they'd experienced at the family dinner on their first night was present. The back wall had been pushed open to reveal an adjoining room where another long table had been set up. People he'd never encountered before sat intermixed with Amira's family members.

As they were escorted to their seats, he searched for Amira. When he saw her next to Duak, he pivoted towards her.

Calvin grabbed his arm and steered him in their original direction. "Calm your ass down. Obviously, this is some sort of celebration. If you create a scene, they'll kick you out of Bagumi and forbid you to ever see her again."

His nostrils flared as he attempted to shake off the anger of seeing her with that prick. He had to remember whose world he currently resided in. Not that it would help if Duak attempted to hurt her in any way. He'd risk banishment to keep Amira safe.

He maintained sight of her once he'd been seated. Duak caught his gaze and exposed his teeth by lifting one side of his mouth before turning and whispering in Amira's ear. She shirked away as she looked in Jake's direction.

Jake went to stand.

Calvin pushed him down by the shoulder. "Do I need to tie you to the chair? Or make our excuses and leave? The man is just trying to goad you. Don't fall for it."

Before he could utter a word, a sudden hush fell over the crowd.

The king had gotten to his feet. "Tonight, we celebrate. The kingdoms of Bagumi and Ashani will unite in marriage. Just as our children will become one, so will our lands, ensuring the growth of our prosperity." The people clapped. "On this day, a betrothal has been made that will change the future of our kingdoms."

Jake's body stiffened with dread. He knew that whatever the king said next would change his life forever. Staring in Amira's direction, he attempted to catch her gaze. Her refusal to look anywhere but at the table with her lips in a straight line and shoulders drawn back confirmed his suspicions.

"In one month, my youngest daughter, Princess Amira Oware Saene, will marry Prince Duak Omiata of Ashani, joining our kingdoms."

The diner's cheers were deafening as Jake attempted to make sense of what he'd just heard. Amira and the monarch from Hell were to be married? When had this been arranged? Had she known about it the whole time? Is that why she'd been worried last night after the party? She must've known she couldn't get out of the situation.

He gripped the edge of the table as his chest tightened, making breathing difficult. Had she used him to have a last fling before getting married? Did she love him at all? The questions pounded in his head until it throbbed.

He looked for answers in Amira's beautiful face. While she perused the crowd, a small, tight smile was all she wore as her eyes sparkled. In anger. Her eyes had reflected the same defiance last night as she'd dealt with Duak.

And then, her gaze caught his. It took nothing but the slightest shake of her head to soothe his inner turmoil, and his headache disappeared. He nodded in response, and a real smile lit her face, even reaching her eyes.

Mine. Amira belonged with him, and nothing else mattered. Not even the announcement proclaimed by her father. There remained no doubt in his heart, soul, and mind that she would marry no one else but him.

The decibel level in the room decreased as the servers came around to distribute heaping plates of food. Jake's appetite had disappeared, so he ate very little as Calvin attempted to distract him with conversation he couldn't get into. His focus remained on Amira and how they would get her out of the situation she'd obviously been forced into.

By the end of the dinner, he had a plan. Of course, he might get shot by one of the security officers before and maybe even after they implemented it. But he was willing to take the risk if Amira would agree to the scheme.

The dinner dragged, becoming boorishly aggravating the longer she sat next to Duak. There was nothing her father enjoyed more than to celebrate one of his proclamations.

She'd been surrounded by women, some she knew, and others she wished she'd never met for the past few hours. The commotion hadn't required her input. The queens had already taken over her life, and she detested it. Although she hadn't had a moment to herself, she'd mentally outlined a plan that settled her riotous emotions.

Oftentimes, the simplest ideas worked the best. She'd take her grievance straight to her father, pleading, if necessary, to revoke the marriage arrangement.

Her business degree had helped her to come up with alternate ways to seal the agreement they'd struck in a more modern manner. One that wouldn't need the sacrifice of her future happiness in order to bind the countries.

She hadn't had the chance to speak to her father yet. She'd always known him to be a fair and just man. A loving and caring father. What he'd done was tantamount to betrayal in her eyes. He'd played her as a pawn of the throne in order to appease others without considering her feelings.

Now, she regretted never telling anyone about Duak's behaviour as a child. Her father wouldn't have allowed the betrothal if he'd known just what a despicable excuse for a human being the prince truly was. She'd inform him soon enough.

She'd never marry Duak. Especially not when the owner of her heart had claimed her.

Jake was the only reason the dinner had been tolerable. When his scowl had disappeared and his knuckles regained colour when he'd released the edge of the table, she'd been sure he'd understood her non-verbal message that she hadn't known about the betrothal. At least, she hoped the slight nod he'd given indicated understanding. If she were in his shoes, betrayal would've been the first thing to come to her mind.

Did he know her well enough to realize that she'd never intentionally hurt another person? Especially him, the man who'd helped her keep her sanity when she'd been lonely in that cold foreign land? If she hadn't met him, she may have forgone completing her masters and run back home.

"My family will be returning to Ashani tomorrow, but I will remain here," Duak said as he cut into his lamb fillet. "I do not trust you with the outsider."

She didn't bother to respond.

The man gnawed on the meat and swallowed before narrowing his eyes at her. "You are not to speak to him again. I will ensure it."

Her head roasted with ire at his impertinence. How could one gutless man irk her to the point of wanting to commit violence against him? The fact that she allowed herself to react to any of his useless words galled her even more.

She kept quiet. The dinner wouldn't last forever.

"If—" he said the word with a sharpness in his voice, "—I learn on our wedding night that you are not pure, I will punish you. Severely."

How dare he? She barred her teeth in what many would consider a rather scary smile. She maintained her silence with the strength of will it had taken to learn how to dance on the tips of her toes in ballet. It wouldn't be her family who was placed into shame this night.

From the corner of her eye, she saw him smirk.

"Already, you are learning to obey me. A compliant, quiet wife is what I will have in my home. Someone who will bring peace to my palace and contentment to my loins. It may take time, but you will submit to my commands."

She'd had more than enough.

Although not a look she'd ever practiced in the mirror, she knew that her upper lip curled into a sharp snarl, chin jutted out, nostrils flaring, veins distended with the tension in her neck, and eyes throwing sparks so intense she feared setting her home on fire, would convey her full fury. Satisfied when his head jerked and he grimaced, she growled so only he could hear.

"If you ever speak to me in such a manner again, I will ensure with my very own hands that you will not be able to walk the next day. You are a more delusional arse than I thought if you believe that you can *tame* me in any way. If you want a passive woman, then you should go for one. It's not too late."

Not yet done and enjoying his wide-eyed, stunned expression, she plastered on a smile just in case anyone was watching. "No matter how much you manipulated the situation to suit you, know that I will not marry you. There is no goodness in you, and I refuse to be shackled to such an evil man."

Lifting the napkin from her lap, she folded it instead of slapping it across his face. She spoke her next words loudly enough for others at their table to hear.

"I'm overjoyed to the point of exhaustion at our upcoming nuptials, my prince. Kindly excuse me so that I may rest. I'd like to be fresh and alert enough tomorrow to begin planning for our wedding."

Placed in the position where he couldn't decline her request, he gave a curt nod. He didn't even have the decency to offer to walk her to her room. After she'd just put the fear of Saene in him, she didn't blame him. Getting to her feet, she noticed him signal someone. She looked up to find a pretty woman wearing a simple black dress heading in her direction.

"Your comfort is my greatest concern, so until I can have you under my roof in Ashani where I can pamper and protect you with greater ease, I have assigned one of my cousins to escort you and take care of you for the next three days while we remain in Bagumi."

Her eye twitched several times. He had no idea of the claw-baring beast he'd awakened in her. She sat again, lowered her gaze from his, in what others would presume as deference, and once again raised her voice. "You are generous, Prince Duak, but my family has always been able to cater to my needs."

The people around her agreed with grumbles.

"I meant no insult to your family."

She cocked her head to meet his gaze. "And yet, you have delivered one."

His face underwent a strange contortion reflecting first confusion and then anger. "I apologize," he gritted through his teeth.

The smile she gave to the people around her was genuine. "I accept your apology. And since we are agreed that I am both safe and comfortable in my own home, kindly inform your cousin to remain in the dining area and enjoy her meal."

As if he'd known trouble was brewing, Zareb stepped to her side. "Is everything all right here?"

"Of course." She added a tinkle of laughter as she stood next to her brother. "I was just telling Prince Duak how my family enjoys spoiling me with their care."

Zareb towered over Duak and glared down at him with his eyes narrowed and lips thinned, knowing that the man might urinate in his seat. Duak gulped and averted his gaze.

Her brother directed his words towards her while maintaining his wide-legged stance in Duak's direction. "Yes, as the youngest in the family, no one will ever see harm come to you. The consequences will make the offender wish he were only being tortured."

Coward that he was, Duak shrivelled into his seat rather than defend himself against Zareb's not so veiled threat. The rest of the table remained quiet and attentive although a few jaws had dropped.

Zareb held out his arm to her while still staring at Duak.

She placed her hand in the crook of his arm. "Have a good night," she said in a pleasant voice, more to those at the table rather than Duak.

He could choke on the rest of his food, for all she cared. It would make her life infinitely easier if he did. Then, she recanted the ill thought. After all, someone in the world loved him. It would just never be her.

CHAPTER THIRTEEN

Hands fisted at her sides, Amira bit the edge of her tongue to keep the tirade at bay as they marched away from the dining room.

Zareb stepped out of arms' reach.

"I didn't find out about the betrothal until you did this afternoon. Father called me in with the rest of the family, asking me to bring a few of our low-key security." He rubbed the hair on his chin. "Looking back, I think they may have been to possibly contain you."

Although stern, her brother always knew how to make her smile.

"I would never have embarrassed the family. Having Mama present was all the security that was needed." The frown returned to her face. "Did you see how happy she was?"

His dreadlocks swayed as he shook his head. "I don't think she was."

"I'm not talking about the part where they whisk me away in three days," she clarified. "But the marriage contract itself."

"I knew what you meant. I think she put on a show for the outsider's sake."

"She's not that good at masking her feelings."

"Believe what you want, Amira, but I've given you my opinion."

How could she deny what she'd seen with her own eyes? Her mother wanted the match. "You obviously weren't happy."

Zareb stopped walking and looked at her. "Even when it doesn't seem like it, I always have your best interest at heart. Duak is not good for you."

It had to be the most emotional thing he'd ever said to her. With a lightened heart, she hugged her brother. "Thank you. Now, all I have to do is get Baba to believe it."

The sound of feet rapidly pounding along the marble caught their attention.

Amira released her brother and flung herself into Jake's open arms as joy flooded her. His belief in her brought a relief she'd never felt before as she rested her head against his broad chest. For the first time since learning about the engagement, she completely let go of the dread that had tormented her. His strong hands rubbing her back both soothed and aroused.

Gaining emotional control, she stepped out of his embrace just in case someone came strolling down the hall.

"I didn't know," she rushed out, needing him to understand the whole story. "My father announced it this afternoon when I was summoned to his office. And then, the women swept me away with their excitement and kept me with them the whole time so that I couldn't contact you. I won't marry the brute. I refuse. Even if I wasn't in love with you, I still wouldn't."

Jake's penetrating blue eyes smiled along with his lips. "I believe you."

She placed a hand over her mouth as her throat became thick with gratitude and relief. She swallowed hard. "Good, because it's the truth."

Just as she was about to once again ignore that they were in a public area of the palace and cup his cheek, another set of footfalls reached them. This time much slower, yet authoritative.

She half-expected to see Duak striding up to them. Instead, one of the security guards greeted them as he went along his evening rounds. Zareb gave him a few rapid-fire instructions before the group took off towards the guest quarters.

In the suite, Jake took her hand and led her to the couch. Calvin and Zareb settled into the adjacent armchairs.

"What's going to happen now?" he asked.

She'd been thinking about it since getting over the shock of the news. "I'll talk to my father in the morning. He has to see reason."

Amira caught Zareb's deepened scowl. "What? Don't you think Baba will reverse the decision once he knows what kind of man Duak is? He could easily come up with another solution for binding our countries that doesn't involve marrying me off. I've come up with a couple. They're good, too."

"I don't know. I understand the political side of our father a lot better than you. Sometimes, I think he'd put the kingdom over everything. Even his family. The Ashani have been restless for years. This is the chance to settle our dispute in a peaceful manner." He held out his hands and laced his fingers together. "Marriage seals families together. Even though he may not like giving you away after he discovers Duak's true nature, I don't doubt that he'll keep his promise and marry you off, anyway."

Amira crossed her arms over her chest as a protective ward to his words. She refused to believe their father could be so heartless towards his own flesh and blood. He loved and wanted the best for them. Didn't he? Would he really put the kingdom over her personal happiness? "I don't think he'd be so cruel." She hated that her words had come out with a quiver.

"He loves me," she said with more confidence.

Zareb shrugged. "That's true, but I want you to be ready for the likelihood of him insisting on you going through with the marriage even though he knows you don't agree."

Her brother certainly knew how to kick a person when they were down with his tough love. Fortunately, she wasn't ready to stay on the ground. Ready to fight for what she knew was right. To claim her life as her own. She nodded once with conviction. "He'll listen to me. I know he will. He has to change his mind, because there's no way I'm marrying him."

"Because you're marrying me."

Everyone turned to stare at Jake.

Her brows slammed together. Had she heard him correctly? "What?"

He cleared his throat, and his Adam's apple bobbed as he clasped her hands. "I know you better than any other woman I've ever met. I've shared things with you that not even Calvin knows, and you've never judged me. I knew long before stepping foot in your presence that we belong together. That I had fallen irrevocably in love with you and wanted you in my life. Forever."

He stood and left her side before she could snap out of her surprised state and respond.

"I'll be right back."

Overwhelmed by his impassioned speech, she finally let herself blink. Did he really want to marry her? More than anything else in the world, she wanted to be his wife.

The three of them remained quiet. Not even Calvin had a sarcastic comment for the moment. She garnered the courage to look at her brother. As usual, his expression was unreadable. What was he thinking? Did he approve of the love match she'd made with a foreigner?

She didn't have time to ask as Jake rushed back into the room. He knelt on one knee while bending the other. Amira clutched at her chest to keep her heart from exploding. Was this really happening? "Jake, what are you doing?"

Calvin's "Oh, boy," couldn't be missed.

"Amira, you're the most extraordinary woman I've ever met. Even if this situation hadn't created the urgency, I would've still asked you to marry me while I was in Bagumi." He flipped over his hand to reveal a ring box. When he opened it, a gorgeous, round diamond accented with four smaller emerald-cut diamonds as side stones glimmered up at her. "Will you marry me?"

Her mouth opened and closed as she struggled to get her vocal cords to work. He'd come to her country already in love. Ready to spend the rest of his life with her. Her feelings for him had just grown exponentially. Only a fool would turn him down. "Yes."

It took a moment for the simply stated answer to penetrate. When it did, Jake jumped up, bringing her along as he kissed her hard on the lips. "Yes?"

She nodded and laughed. "Definitely. As long as you're sure."

Settling her down, he held her by the shoulders. "I've never been surer of anything in my life." When he leaned in, the kiss held an unmistakable promise she'd never experienced before.

The clearing of someone's throat broke them apart.

She looked over her shoulder to find Zareb with his head bent. She held onto Jake's arm when the need for her brother's approval caused her to sway. Did he disapprove of her heart's choice? Would he cause a problem?

When he straightened, his cheeks rose with a full smile. He stepped closer. "Congratulations."

She hugged him, immeasurably grateful for his support. Zareb had a tendency to analyse everything and brooked absolutely no nonsense. His approval meant the world to her.

"Thank you," she whispered, her throat clogged.

When he released her, he offered a hand to her fiancé who shook it.

"I know I don't have to give you the speech about me hunting you down like a deer needed for meat during a time of starvation if you disappoint my sister."

Jake shook his head, and to his credit, maintained a smile while holding Zareb's gaze. "No, you don't. I'll treat her as precious for the rest of my life."

Amira's hand fluttered to her throat at the sweetness of the exchange.

Calvin smacked Jake on the back before swooping in for a hug. "Congratulations, buddy."

"Thanks."

And then, Calvin kissed her on the cheek before embracing her. "What site did you two meet on again?"

She laughed, went to Jake, and settled into his side with arms wrapped around his waist to make sure she didn't transcend to the sky with the helium-like lightness which had filled her.

"With all of this celebrating," Jake said, "let's not forget that you're still engaged to Duak by edict of the king."

The elation of the moment had optimism pumping through her veins. "Father will negate it all. I just know it."

Zareb's expression had returned to indecipherable. "And if he doesn't?"

"He will," she insisted.

Her future depended on it.

CHAPTER FOURTEEN

Zareb had insisted on Amira returning to her room. She'd spent all night on the phone with Jake. They'd talked about so much, but both seemed to avoid the topic of where they would live once they got married.

Anxiety settled in her stomach at the thought of leaving her family and friends in Bagumi. Her overseas experience in Switzerland had opened her eyes to just how much she depended on them. She'd marinated in a slight depression while she'd been away. Even with the security guard they'd assigned to be with her, and talking to her family every chance she got, she'd almost failed at her life of independence outside of Bagumi.

Nothing had gone as well for her in Switzerland as it did when she was in the bosom of her homeland. That was until she started talking to Jake. His virtual presence in her life had turned everything around.

Would the same loneliness she'd experienced during her time abroad threaten to suffocate her if she left Bagumi again, even with Jake as her husband? Did she have the courage to find out, or would she rather convince him to stay? Would he if she asked? Would her family accept him?

The questions of doubt threatened to give her a headache now that the adrenaline from the thrill of becoming engaged to Jake had dwindled. She forced herself to focus on the imminent meeting with her father. Although both Jake and Zareb had offered to talk to him with her, she had declined. She needed to be strong and handle the situation on her own, showing her father that she was mature enough to make her own decisions.

Amira patted her head to make sure her dreads still remained in the updo before knocking on the door of her father's apartment.

An unpretentious man despite his powerful position, her father opened the door and then his arms to hug his last born. She soaked in his love. With two wives, seven children, and a kingdom to run, she didn't spend as much time with him as she'd like and appreciated the occasions she could.

"Come in and sit, Amira," he said in their language.

She responded in her mother tongue as the whole conversation would be spoken. "Thank you, Baba."

After they had settled on the couch, he smiled. "You will be the first of my children to marry. I am very happy. Duak is a good man, and you were friends when growing. The match is a strong one."

Amira held back her wince of disagreement. He was so proud about the accomplishment he'd made. Her heart hurt at having to disappoint him after being such an obedient child. As far as he knew, anyway. All of the tact she'd learned over the years flew out the window as she blurted out the truth.

"Baba, I'm in love with another man and would like to marry him."

The admission didn't make her feel as good as she thought it would. His response was all that mattered, and now, she wasn't sure if he'd agree to her scheme. She hated that she now doubted her own self-esteem. The unfamiliar feeling made butterflies flitter in her stomach. Having never been in the position to directly defy her father, she wrung her hands as she waited for his reaction.

He stroked his beard. "I see."

Her lungs burned while she held her breath during the time he took to deliberate the information she'd flung at him all while wanting to run away.

"It is the foreigner," he stated with a hint of a question.

"Yes, Baba. We have known each other for a year and have fallen in love." She gained strength by touching the engagement ring hanging on a chain lying over her heart. "He has asked me to marry him."

Her greatest role model stared at her before nodding. "Why did you not tell me this before?"

Hope rose. "I wanted to be sure before I announced our relationship."

"And are you?"

"Yes, Baba."

Air wheezed into his nose before he released it on a grunt as he stood and walked to the other side of the room. He returned to the same spot he'd vacated. "The agreement is signed and binding. You will marry Duak and unite our two countries."

She blinked, not believing the edict he'd given. Again.

"But Baba," she protested, not able to keep the pain from her voice. "I don't like Duak. I find him to be unkind and controlling." Her voice wavered as her throat tightened and tears filled her eyes. "I won't enjoy being married to him. Don't you wish me to be happy?"

"Who is to say you will not? In time, you will learn to like him, and if the fates are kind, you may grow to love him. He is fond of you. He has spoken of it many times, and I, as a father, not a king, believe he will treat you well."

Her mind spun with confusion as she struggled to find something to make him change his mind. If she didn't, her life would be ruined. "Baba, he is a cruel man. I have experienced it several times when we were growing up."

Her father laughed. The sound she loved now raked against her ears. "You cannot compare the actions of a child to that of a man. He has become honourable. He will inherit the throne, and you will be queen of Ashani. Many long to be in your position, and you have been chosen."

Despair slaughtered the hope she'd held as the white handkerchief she wiped along her cheeks turned brown from her makeup and tears. "But I don't want to be queen. I would prefer to be the wife of a man who loves and respects me in return. Jake is a good, educated, hard-working man."

"Of this, I am aware. Yet, he is neither wealthy nor of royal blood or stature. You have received every luxury you have ever desired. I doubt he would be able to provide the same. Most importantly, he cannot stabilize the relationship between us and the Ashani like the marriage between you and Duak. The decision has been made, and I cannot go back on my word. It is final. You will marry Duak in one month."

Blinking and shaking her head, she didn't believe him. She couldn't accept that he'd just prosecuted her to a life of misery. This couldn't be happening. Did her life really not matter to him? This couldn't be happening. He had to listen. To change his mind. To prove that he loved her. Flinging herself to the floor, she rested her head against his thigh and pleaded. "Please Baba, do not make me marry him. Please. I beg of you."

The words of desperation ended as she sobbed in earnest.

Her father patted her head. "Get up, my daughter. You are a princess of the Royal House of Saene. You do not beg, not even to the king."

Of course, he only cared about her status. Not the trauma he'd inflicted to his youngest daughter. She struggled onto the seat and attempted to get her bawling under control. When she was left with sniffling and choppy breaths, her father spoke again.

"I had a conversation with Duak before the agreement was made. He promised to treat you well. He is aware of how much I love my children and seek the best for them." His face hardened. "No one would dare cross me for fear of the repercussions."

His explanation didn't release the vise gripping her heart. She had to fight the decision. Make him see reason. "But... doesn't my happiness... mean anything... to you?"

Her father's dark eyes stared into hers. "With time, you will forget about the feelings you have for this foreigner. You will appreciate the life Duak will provide for you. That of a queen. You are one of my most resourceful and adaptive offspring, and I know that no matter where you find yourself, you will be successful. Anything you seek to have and do, you will."

She closed her eyes for a moment in an attempt to restrain her heartbreak. Her tears of desolation and lying at his feet begging for his reconsideration hadn't touched him.

Finally, she opened her eyes to the realization that nothing would make him change his mind.

How had her father gotten so brainwashed by Duak? Why hadn't she come forward about his horrid behaviour years ago? Would it have made a difference?

Zareb had been right. Her father put the needs of the kingdom before even those of his children.

It would do no good to try and convince him. His mind was made up.

So was hers.

She held her head up high and pulled her shoulders back, reclaiming her dignity. "Thank you, Baba."

What more could she say through the disappointment clogging her throat? She would figure a way out of the engagement without her father's help. Having Duak kidnapped and sent to Siberia came to mind, but she dismissed it outright. Not that she wouldn't mind him freezing his toes off, but the logistics of getting him there would be a nightmare.

"It is well, my daughter. Remember that my love for you transcends everything and will never change. Whatever happens will be for the better."

No longer inclined to believe the words he'd spoken often, she gained no reassurance. Amira hugged her father, understanding that it may be one of the last opportunities she'd ever have. She wouldn't marry Duak. Defying the king's order would garner consequences which may separate her from her family. Forever.

CHAPTER FIFTEEN

As soon as Jake had opened the door, Amira had tackled him with the force of a line-backer during a blitz. She'd clung to him crying ever since.

Her inconsolable sobbing had unnerved him to the point of wanting to call Zareb, but he'd held off. As her man, he wanted to be the one to ease her pain. To have protected her from it in the first place, but he hadn't. So now, he sat with her on his lap and rocked while speaking words he hoped would bring comfort.

After a tortuous fifteen minutes of attempting to soothe her, the weeping abated, and she began to hiccup in between her sniffles. Unwilling to release her limp frame, he lifted her when he stood. She held onto him with confidence, which swelled his pride, as he went to the kitchen for a bowl of sugar before returning to the living room couch and sitting. Opening the small container he used to sweeten his coffee in the morning, he took a pinch between his fingers.

"Open your mouth."

When her red-rimmed, puffy eyes looked up at him, his heart hurt for her. He hated seeing her so miserable, but was glad he'd been the one she'd sought. "The sugar will get rid of your hiccups."

She opened her mouth, and he dropped the crystals into her mouth. After a moment, the hiccups were gone, and she gave him a watery smile. "Thank you. Where did you learn that?"

"A fictional book I read last year."

She rested her head against his shoulder and sniffled. "My father refused to end the engagement."

He'd figured as much. He'd gotten an idea about the man from the way she'd spoken with pride about her father over the past year. She'd emphasized how he ruled the country with a firm, yet compassionate hand. After Zareb's doubtful reaction to her plan of approaching the king, he'd been ready for the rejection of her proposal. Although he'd held out hope that her father would relent, it hadn't been enough for the negative reaction to devastate him like it had her.

Stroking her back, he laid a kiss on her forehead and remained silent.

"It was as if he didn't care how I felt about the whole thing. That it didn't matter if I was happy or not, just as long as I married that arse in order to keep the peace."

Her eyes had filled with more tears when she looked up at him. "My father doesn't love me."

"Sweetheart, you know that's not true."

She bit her quivering bottom lip as she took in stuttering breaths. "Not enough to risk a war."

"Well, I can see how that could be an issue. I don't agree with your father not allowing you to choose your own future, but I can understand the tough position he's been placed in."

He put a finger against her lips when she opened her mouth to speak. "From what you've told me about him, he's an honourable and good man. He's made a promise. For an upright person, they're not easy to get out of. Tell me exactly what happened."

By the time Amira had finished the story, she was crying again.

"Now you see that he doesn't love me. He called me resourceful and adaptive and said I could live anywhere." She reached for a tissue and blew her nose.

"I'm sure no one could survive in the depths of Hell where he wants to send me."

His woman had a flair for the dramatic. He was sure the royal palace of Ashani could compete with Bagumi in luxury. There, she'd receive the treatment she'd become accustomed to, unlike the simplicity he could provide. But he'd die before letting Duak get his manipulating claws on her. The prince didn't deserve her. Jake realized that neither did he, but she loved him, anyway.

"There's only one thing we can do," he said.

She sat up and gripped a handful of his shirt in each hand. "We can't kill Duak. His family would be too upset."

His head jerked back at the violent response so unlike the woman he'd gotten to know.

And then, she giggled. "I'm just kidding. Well, mostly. What's your great idea?"

"We elope."

She scrambled off his lap to a standing position before he could hold her in place. Eyes wide and arms akimbo, she stared down at him. "Are you serious?"

Her reaction wasn't anywhere as enthusiastic as he'd expected, but it didn't deter him. He got to his feet. "Yes. I don't even want to imagine what life would be like without you in it."

Grabbing her hands, he appreciated just how strong and capable they were. "I asked you to be my wife yesterday, and you said yes. If you marry me, then your father can't force you to marry Duak." He paused, and his eyes widened. "Unless you practice polyandry here."

She blinked up at him for a moment. When she seemed to understand, she giggled. "Would you be willing to allow me to marry another man?"

"Hell no!"

That had her laughing. "To the best of my knowledge, it isn't practiced in Bagumi. By the way, if you think you're marrying more than me, you have another think coming." Her finger poking his shoulder emphasized her point.

"Sweetheart, I have a feeling that you're all I'll ever desire."

Instead of melting, or throwing her arms around him, she nodded. "I'd better be."

He grinned and kissed her cheek. She'd definitely be more than enough for him.

"Back to eloping," he said. "What does it matter if we have a big wedding or a small quick ceremony as long as we get to be together?"

Her eyes glistened. This time, the tears were accompanied by a smile. His heart raced at her incredible beauty. She released his hands, stood on her toes, and peppering his face with kisses. He smiled, taking her fervent response to be affirmative. And then, her mouth settled on his.

Heat burgeoned low in his belly as she slipped her tongue inside his mouth. No one had ever made him feel as alive. All he wanted to do was absorb her whole.

He slid his hands along her ribs, his thumbs brushing along the sides of her full breasts. He cupped them before focusing on her nipples. Her moans as they pebbled took over all reason. Bending, he placed one arm under her knees and the other behind her back and lifted her. She wound her arms around his neck with a squeal.

Her glazed eyes cleared as she looked up at him. The heat in her dark brown eyes drove him to take a step towards his room. She stopped him with a hand on his chest. Would she say no?

She pointed towards the second bedroom. "Where's Calvin?"

For him, it didn't matter if the palace's whole security team were in the suite as he made love to her. "He went exploring with a guard."

An uncharacteristic shy smile as she lowered her lids concerned him.

"Does this mean we'll have to be quick?"

She jiggled in his arms as he chuckled.

"Not at all." He kissed her lips. "I've waited all of my life for you, Amira. And I'll have you in it for the rest of my days. If you'll allow, I'd like to make love to you. To show you with my body just how much I love you. To please you. I'll make—"

His words were cut off when she took advantage of his open lips by pressing hers to his and caressing the inside of his mouth. The bold movements of her exploration threatened to send them toppling to the floor as his knees wobbled. Strengthening his hold on her, he walked to the bedroom, closed the door, and stood her on her feet.

He tugged at the flesh of her ear with his teeth before whispering, "I have protection."

She pushed her chest against his with a low groan. "Me, too. Only mine is in my bag on the couch."

She nibbled the skin of his neck, and he forgot the track of the conversation.

Her jasmine and lemon scent seeped into his nostrils as he returned to her lips to sample their sweetness. His initial desire to take things slowly transitioned as their hands moved in a frenzied hurry to send clothes skittering to the floor.

He left her for the briefest of moments to get the condoms from his bag. Opening the pack, he took one out, tore the wrapper open, and slid it on. The way she'd watched the process with her bottom lip between her teeth and her nipples pointed right at him had gotten him impossibly harder. When he returned to her, they lay on the bed together.

"I fell in love with your personality, sense of humour, intelligence, kindness, and encouraging nature, but I must admit that your face and body are absolutely gorgeous."

She thanked him for the compliment by reaching between them and stroking him. He sucked in air through his teeth as he shifted his hips away from her exquisite torture. Her pleasure was his main priority.

Starting at her neck, he kissed along the dip at her collar bone. He took his time nipping the skin along her arms until he reached her fingers. He placed three of her digits in his mouth and sucked. Her moan drove him insane with need. Releasing the fingers, he continued with the glorious exploration over her belly and then down her toned legs. He reversed direction and kissed his way up her until he met her lips. Their kiss was slow and deep.

He touched his hand to her core and groaned at her slick heat as he delved a finger inside of her tightness. Her legs widened as he slipped in a second finger while taking one hard nipple into his mouth and teasing it.

"Yes, Jake."

Encouraged by her hips bucking up to meet his probing fingers, he curved the digits as he stroked. Her arched back pressed her perfect breast further into his face. He suckled at the nipple before blowing on it. "You like that?"

Her only answer was a whimper as he slid his fingers out of her and inched back in. His thumb found her clit, and he strummed the bundle of nerves as he pulled the other dark peak of her succulent breast into his mouth. The bite of her nails into the skin of his shoulder heightened his pleasure as he continued with his double onslaught.

"I need you inside, Jake. Please."

He eased his fingers out and poised himself over her. Looking into her eyes, he took his time sinking into her. Nothing had ever felt so right.

Her legs and arms wrapped around him, bringing them closer as they moved together with a slow rhythm.

"Jake," came as a plea as she arched into him.

The intensity increased as he kissed her. His hips pumped harder and faster as he revelled in the heat of her mouth.

When she began to tighten and pulse around him, he reached down and rubbed her nipple between his fingers. Her scream entered his mouth as her orgasm hit. His wasn't far behind as he lifted her leg higher against his hip and stroked even deeper into her.

His explosion left him drained and weak, but happier than he'd ever been. Lying to the side of her, he struggled to breathe. Her chest rose and fell with her pants.

When she turned and their gazes met, he raised his head and brushed her lips with a soft kiss. She laid a palm against his cheek as she kissed him back.

When she pulled away, her smile made his heart tremble. "That was...amazing."

The word didn't begin to describe what they'd just shared, but he'd accept it. "Definitely."

She shook her head. "I've never..."

In shock, he propped himself onto his elbow. She hadn't been a virgin; he'd have felt it. Wouldn't he? She'd displayed no pain when he'd entered her. Had her moan not been one of pleasure? "Was that your first time?"

"It might as well have been."

He let out a breath of relief even as disappointment hit him. He didn't like the fact that someone else had touched her first, and yet, he couldn't offer her his virginity, either. He pushed his hypocritical thought away.

She drew her lower lip into her mouth. "I didn't think it could be so powerful. Incredible. Out of this world."

They lay languid and silent together before reality returned.

He kissed her bare shoulder. "We need to get dressed."

She stroked her hand along his chest and down his stomach, reawakening his still sheathed member. "Or we could do it again."

He pulled her closer and then kissed her hard on the lips. "I promise we will, but soon, we won't be alone."

Before she could roll off the bed, he looked her in the eyes. "I love you, Amira."

Her slow grin made his stomach flip. "I love you, too, Jake."

They got cleaned up and dressed. His life after being with Amira had changed forever. How in the world did he get so lucky to find her? All he knew was that he'd do anything to keep her by his side. Anything.

CHAPTER SIXTEEN

Amira had never seen blood drain from a person's face before. She reached out and grabbed Jake's hand, worried that she'd driven him into a state of physical shock. "Are you okay?"

His nod didn't convince her, so she went to the kitchenette and removed a can of juice before going back to him. Opening it, she perched it at his mouth. "Drink."

The sound of gulping filled the room as he emptied the can.

Making love had been the most intense experience of her life. She's never known the act could be so all-encompassing. Not that she had an abundance of experience with sex, but the guy she'd snuck out of the palace to be with at nineteen hadn't come close to delivering what Jake had.

They'd dressed and returned to the living room. She'd found it important that he understood the consequences of breaking her father's decree of marrying Duak, so she'd listed the ones she knew. When she'd mentioned death as a true possibility at disobeying the command of the king, his face had gone pale.

By the time he'd placed the can down, colour had returned to his skin, but the enthusiasm she'd felt moments ago had diminished. Who would want to risk their life for love when they had their whole future in front of them?

"I understand if you no longer want to elope. It's too much to ask of anyone." She swallowed hard. "I'll find a way out of marrying Duak without getting us both into trouble."

"I never said I didn't want to. You just stunned me with the news." He stood, walked around the couch, and returned to sit on the other side of her.

Odd how this action reminded her so much of her father.

"I doubt that your father would have me killed. Not even imprisonment. I may not be on the political radar in the US, but my country is a force to be reckoned with and wouldn't tolerate the murder, not even as an official punishment by the government. I'm sure your father understands this."

She didn't bring up past incidences of horrible punishments, such as canings, doled out to US citizens while in other lands. His government had not been able to do anything to help those people.

He grabbed her hands and squeezed. "I'm more worried about how eloping will affect you."

His concern touched her in a deeper place than she knew existed. "I don't know. This has never happened before. None of my siblings has gotten married or undergone an edict so life-changing."

"Any ideas, though?"

Her eyes watered at the worst conceivable consequence. "Banishment from Bagumi."

His tanned skin took on a reddened hue as his upper lip curled into a snarl. "That's not right! Why don't you have the option of making your own decision when it comes to such an important aspect of your life?"

She shrugged. "I thought we did...until yesterday."

"But you don't always follow the rules."

She grinned, recalling times she'd been disobedient. "My parents raised us to be strong-willed and have our own opinions even though they expected us to obey their rules. I believe they wanted us to always consider options and make the right choice."

His stormy dark blue eyes stared into hers. "And what's best for you in this situation?"

Did he really have to ask? Even if death were to be her own punishment, she'd still make the same choice. "To marry you."

The fingers he stroked against her cheek held callouses. The hand of a man who wasn't afraid of or unwilling to work. "And give up your family? Your access to luxury? The chance at being a queen one day?"

She grasped his wrist. Partly to keep him touching her and partly to anchor herself with his strength. Being able to lean on him during this difficult time meant more than she'd ever be able to convey. "I love my family. They've been all I've ever known, but from that first interaction with you, I recognized how special you were and that we'd be friends. When I initially saw you in Zawadi's office, the world disappeared. I mean literally. It might sound crazy, but at that moment, I knew you were mine." She tapped the centre of her chest. "Heart, body, and soul. Mine." She paused so he'd have no doubt about her decision. "I choose you, Jake."

His eyes shone. Instead of responding with words, he merged their lips in a kiss of possessiveness that she returned with equal fervour. When he pulled back, he rested their foreheads together as their breaths mingled.

"I love you so much, Amira." He licked his lips and then sighed. "I wish things could've been different. I don't want to be the cause of angst between you and your family, but how do we elope?"

She propelled herself onto him with so much force that he released an "Oomph."

"I have no idea, but we'll figure it out."

They had no other choice.

***

Much to Amira's overheated body's disappointment, Calvin's return ten minutes later prevented them from returning to the bedroom. Instead of rediscovering the pleasure Jake could induce in her, they'd been forced to discuss the details of the elopement.

Having Calvin's analytical mind involved helped. The tentative plan they came up with would be implemented in two days, before she was taken to Ashani. She'd sneak out of her beloved country alone while Jake and Calvin stayed behind—they'd leave a day or so later. It had taken a lot of convincing to get Jake to agree. Just in case she wasn't able to get away, at least they wouldn't be caught with her.

The risk of discovery was too great for them to attempt getting married while in Bagumi. Her status prevented it. Jake, with his fair skin and blue eyes, was too much of a stranger. No one would dare betray the throne by officiating the ceremony or registering them.

Her complete reserve of confidence had deserted her. The inside of her right cheek became raw with how much she'd chewed on it while seated in Zareb's apartment outside the palace compound. Her brother knew what was stake, but would he help her escape Bagumi without detection? He was as dedicated to the throne as the king himself. Would he be willing to go against their father?

Panic that Zareb would refuse his assistance had her heart pounding, but she could only ask. If he said no, then she'd find another way of getting out of marrying Duak.

Zareb settled plates of fried plantain, bean stew, and grilled fish in front of her and Jake before going for his own food. Sitting across from them at the dining room table, he bowed his head for a few seconds and then forked food into his mouth.

Amira knew that her brother wouldn't converse until he'd finished his meal. A habit that annoyed their mother, who saw mealtime as a chance to catch up on her children's lives.

Fifteen minutes later, with her turbulent stomach unable to eat a single bite while Zareb and Jake left their plates empty, she cleared the dishes from the table and returned to her seat.

Zareb looked between her and Jake.

"I'd like to support you, especially since I think Father is wrong to marry you off to a lizard like Duak. But it isn't possible."

Did he know about their plan? She placed her trembling hands in her lap. "What are you talking about?"

"The reason you're here with Jake. You want to elope."

She blinked up at him several times. She took those seconds to accept that for years, she'd been correct about him. He was clairvoyant. How in the world had he always been in the right place at the right time?

"How did you know?" she asked. "You're psychic aren't you? It's a twin thing, isn't it?"

Zareb actually rolled his eyes. "I'm not psychic, just intuitive, intelligent, and very observant. Who do you think you're dealing with? Father put me in charge of security for a reason."

Jake leaned forward with his eyes narrowed.

"Are my quarters bugged?" His voice got deeper. "Cameras? I swear to God that if—"

Her brother cocked his head as he interrupted with a raised hand. "I like you more every time we meet. You have courage. Something you'll need to be a husband to my sister."

Zareb's rare laughter at his own joke eased the tension in the room.

"You aren't funny," Amira said as she attempted to hide her own smile behind her napkin.

"The man left his home and flew over to Africa not knowing exactly what to expect. All for you." A grin lingered on Zareb's lips. "In a matter of days, you've gotten him to propose and then convinced him to go against our father's pronouncement in order to preserve your relationship."

"It was my idea," Jake said.

Zareb nodded. "And once again, my respect grows. Which is why if I could help, I would. You and Calvin plan to leave the country and take Amira with you somehow because there's no way anyone in this country would allow her to be married without our father's blessing. Not even our enemies would allow it for fear of my father's retribution." He levelled Jake with a stare. "It would be swift and violent."

She shook off the chill trellising down her spine at his warning, and her suspicions rose. "You're wrong. I was going to leave before them." She held back the childish impulse of sticking her tongue out hat him for being right about everything else. He'd never answered Jake's question. "Do you have cameras in the room?"

"No." Zareb tapped his temple. "I just understand people and how they think. My masters in psychology wasn't an automatic pass."

Knowing that her brother never lied, she relaxed into her seat and smiled at Jake who didn't look convinced. "He only ever speaks the truth. My siblings and I have never heard him lie. Or rather caught him in one."

The left corner of Zareb's mouth twerked up.

Why wasn't anything going her way? Amira kept her voice strong even though she wanted to roll on the floor in a tantrum. "So what do we do? I can't marry Duak. It's not an option, and if I travel to Ashani, I'll have absolutely no chance of getting out of the wedding without committing a felony."

"No matter how much I want to help, I cannot and will not go against the throne to help you. Not only do I not want to see you get into trouble, but it would show a blatant disrespect towards Father, which I will not tolerate. Especially not from my baby sister."

They were doomed if he wouldn't help. She slumped into the chair, her shoulders curling forward.

Jake snuck his hand into hers beneath the table and squeezed.

Zareb traced a finger along the wood grain of the table. "I agree with Father that maintaining peace is paramount. Would you want the blood of your countrymen and women on your head?"

For that, she didn't blame her father for not backing out of the marriage. She never had. The threat of war had been the only thing stopping her from publicly refusing to marry Duak. Bagumi and its people meant too much to her. "There has to be a way to save us from violence and still let me be happy."

"I do have an idea," Zareb said.

"What is it?" she and Jake said at the same time.

"There's no one that our Father respects more than his wives. Our mother, especially. If anyone can convince him to change his mind, she can. You know how persuasive Mother is."

Her mother never hesitated to speak her mind about anything she disagreed with. Wouldn't she have protested her only daughter being catapulted to the Ashani without her consent before this if she didn't agree? Or at least talked to her about it?

"I thought you'd come up with something good. Mama would be the last person to help. She married Baba through an arranged marriage. I don't ever recall a conversation where she didn't mention the importance of duty."

She swallowed back the useless need to cry. She'd done enough of that already, and it hadn't helped. "I don't care what you said before, she was happy when Baba made the announcement about the betrothal. One of her children will be the first in the family to wed. And become a queen, no less. She couldn't be more thrilled."

Zareb raised a brow. "Have you spoken to her about it? Is that what she told you? She is both the queen and your mother. Which role do you think is more important to her?"

Amira clutched her chest as the shame hit her. Hard. Unlike her father, her mother had always stood up for them and loved them more than she did her own self. At least, that's what she'd always told them. Would she help if Amira told her about her love for Jake and her desire to marry him? Could her mother's influence change her father's mind and guide him towards finding an alternative solution?

There was only one way to find out. "Will you come with me?"

"No."

She pointed at the love of her life. "What if I bring Jake?"

"Amira, you don't need a buffer. Speaking to her one on one will be best. Tell her your story and listen to hers."

She considered Zareb's words. "What aren't you telling me?"

"Nothing you won't learn soon enough." His narrowed gaze turned to Jake who seemed to be taking everything in as he listened with an attentive ear. "You can let go of her hand now."

Her fiancé's face remained neutral, but he didn't release her. "With all due respect, brother-in-law to be, no thanks."

For the second time that night, Zareb's laughter filled the room.

His Defiant Princess

CHAPTER SEVENTEEN

Amira smoothed sweaty palms down the knee-length dark green skirt her mother had given her as a gift for her last birthday. Why was she so nervous? They'd always had a great relationship. Although she didn't go to her mother with all of her secrets, the woman always listened. Whether she judged or not depended on the indiscretion. And yet, she'd always provided the support her unconditional love promised.

Would she be hurt that Amira hadn't told her about her online relationship with Jake? Or that she'd fallen in love with him and had planned to elope without consulting her?

No need speculating when she'd find out in a few moments, if her father hadn't already told her. She knocked on the door, hoping her mother was home. Unlike with her father, she never had to make an appointment to visit.

The most graceful and beautiful woman she'd ever seen opened the door and pulled her into a tight hug. "Finally, you have come."

The gold brocade ankle-length embroidered dress flowed over a body which didn't look as if it had carried four children. The matching head-tie brought out her high cheekbones, large eyes, and pert nose. Her always-stunning mother led Amira to the couch.

"How long were you going to make me wait?"

Her mind went into overdrive and came out the other side of the question still confused. Did she already know? Best to play dumb. "For what?"

Her mother sighed and waved down a hand. "Never mind. What brings you here?"

Unnerved, she stood and went to the kitchen, pulled out a bottle of juice, and went back to her seat. The drink's coolness seeped into her hands, distracting her momentarily from the task of revealing the biggest secret she'd ever held from her mother.

The queen reached out a hand bearing priceless rings on three out of five fingers and pinched the base of one of Amira's dreads. "Your hair has grown. You need to get them re-twisted."

Of course she'd notice. The woman's own pepper grey dreadlocks were always impeccable. Everything about her was. No matter how good Amira thought she looked, she always felt dowdy when near her. She could never be as beautiful or as poised as the woman who'd given birth to her. "Yes, Mama."

Rather than delve into the reason for her impromptu visit, she opened then took a sip of the mango juice. Perhaps the sugar rush would bolster her courage. She set the bottle on the table and looked at her mother.

"I can't marry Duak. Not just because he's mean and unworthy to even look at me, but because I'm in love with Jake who I met online. We've been talking for about a year, and when he came here, it all just clicked." She sucked in a breath to replenish her lungs.

At her mother's calm expression, she slowed her words. "Baba announced my engagement to Duak. Jake proposed because he said he couldn't see his future without me in it. And now, we want to elope. Zareb says it would be impossible and that I should talk to you about it."

As if she'd run up too many flights of stairs, Amira slumped into the couch, exhausted.

"Why did you think you couldn't come to me?" Her mother's voice held a touch of disappointment.

She hid the regret of not trusting her mother by lowering her gaze. "I didn't want to disappoint you. You were so happy about the engagement. And I wasn't one hundred percent sure about my feelings for Jake until he came to Bagumi." More like ninety-nine percent sure. "Ever since we had a respectful difference in opinion online the first time we encountered each other, not a day has gone by that we haven't communicated. I thought I'd fallen in love with him, but wasn't sure. Who falls in love without meeting the man first?"

Her mother smiled. "Stranger things have happened."

At the quiet response, Amira remembered that she had yet to hear her mother's story, and her curiosity peaked. "I know your marriage with Baba was arranged, but how did it come about?"

"You've never inquired before. Did my youngest son tell you to ask?"

Amira's neck and face heated. "I didn't know there was a story behind it. I just thought you were obedient to your father."

How many times had she practiced the queen's regal tilt of the head and failed to do it half as elegantly?

"You must promise never to reveal to anyone what I'm about to tell you."

Intrigued, Amira placed her right hand over her chest. "I promise."

"It's no secret that I love your father. I always have."

Unable to stop herself, she asked, "Then why did you allow him to marry another woman?"

Instead of a chastisement, her mother smiled. "You've always been the most impatient of my children. I'll get to that. My father, may his soul rest in peace, was not the most reasonable man."

Amira couldn't remember the grandfather who had died when she was three.

"I think you inherited your impetuous and rebellious nature from him," her mother stated with a slight frown. "He didn't look for trouble, but he had a knack for finding it. During his reign, he, like the kings before him, ensured that every able-bodied male, and many females, were soldiers capable of defending their country. He was one of the most feared monarchs in my country's history. He never waged war unless it was absolutely necessary, but always won. A fair man who loved me above all of my five siblings."

"So that's where I get it from?" Amira laughed, and her mother grinned.

"Your father became king at the young age of twenty. A strategist, Ibrahim knew he needed an ally to maintain his throne. He came to my father asking for my hand in marriage in order to align our countries."

Her mother's dark eyes took on a glazed look. "Ibrahim was the most handsome man I had ever seen. I think my eighteen-year-old self fell in love with him at that instant. Little did I know that hormones had taken over, and lust was the actual culprit."

Amira nodded. She'd worried about the same thing when it came to Jake. The difference was that she knew so much about him that love had settled in first. Her hormones had gone berserk when they'd come into physical contact.

"Contrary to other men, your grandfather had married one woman and had loved her with all of his heart. I believe that if it hadn't been for your grandmother's calming influence on her husband, he would've had to fight more battles than he had."

Amira's jaw dropped. How come she'd never known? "I thought men had the right to marry more than one woman."

"They do. Even in my home country way back then, they did. My father chose not to. My parents gave me the ingrained perception of what a marriage should look like." Her mother pointed towards the kitchen. "Get me some water."

Amira jumped up, ran into the kitchen to acquire a bottle from the refrigerator, and rushed back.

After taking a few sips, her mother nodded. "My father was going to refuse Ibrahim's proposal, but I announced that I wanted to marry him."

Disbelieving, she clamped a hand over her mouth. For her entire life, she'd thought her parents had undergone an arranged marriage. Her world had just been shaken as if she'd sat through an earthquake.

"Your grandfather told me that Ibrahim would treat me well, but would take on more wives as time went on. He didn't want that for me. I was young and in love. I was sure he'd fall in love with me and I'd be the only woman your father would ever need."

Tears sprang to her eyes at the unrealistic optimism of a young Princess Zulekha. How much had it hurt her when her father had married another? "Do you regret marrying him?"

"Oh, my precious daughter, no. I couldn't be the love of your father's life, but he's always been mine, and it's been a magnificent experience being with him, even though I had to share. He has given me four incredible children and a life I have loved every moment of."

Feeling like the child she'd been years ago, but not caring, she slid closer to her mother and rested her head against her shoulder. The stress disappeared as her mother kissed her forehead and stroked her hair. Nothing could replace such an eternal, unconditional love.

Her mother broke the silence. "I will help you."

Amira sprang upright. "You will?"

"Of course, you are my daughter. I know you, Amira. I've known you were in love ever since you were in Switzerland."

"You did?"

Her mother laughed. "Yes. There isn't much you can hide from me. I was just waiting for you to come to me. No one would ever accuse me of butting into my children's lives." She winked. "At least not to my face."

Being a woman of power and consequence, she liked to control everything. It showed just how much she respected Amira's independence to not interfere.

"I want the best for you, and I never thought Duak was it. Jake, on the other hand, may not be rich or influential in the worldly sense, but he will treat you with respect all the days of your life. I just have one condition before I get involved."

Barely able to contain her delight, she bounced in her seat. "Name it, and I'll do it."

"It is for Jake."

"He'll do it. I promise."

"We'll see."

The hair at the back of her neck stood on end as a sudden fear grabbed hold of her. The words usually meant *no way in Hell*. She must doubt Jake's ability to comply with whatever she asked of him.

"The year you were in Switzerland was painful for me. I know it was the same for you. I couldn't bear it if you were to move even further to the United States indefinitely."

Why had the room gotten swelteringly hot all of a sudden? Amira licked her upper lip to find it salty.

"Before I help you elope, I need Jake's promise, in writing, that he will move to Bagumi."

Was her mother serious? How could she ask someone to leave his home? She was asking the impossible.

Amira found it difficult to breathe, much less speak. Although they'd never talked about it, she'd decided to be the one to leave home to be with him. And now, her mother was forcing him to either move and be with her, or continue staying in the States and never be together.

Would he be willing to leave everything he knew? His family? His new practice? His home? It wouldn't be easy to adapt from the life he'd lived.

Did he love her enough to give up the only life he'd known?

Her mother had just placed her in a situation where one of them, maybe both, would lose. No matter which decision he took, she hoped that what they gained would be enough.

.

CHAPTER EIGHTEEN

The manner in which Amira twisted her hands and avoided Jake's gaze when he let her in alerted him to the negative feedback she must've received.

Before she could get far, he turned her by the shoulders and wrapped his arms around her. His knees went weak with relief as she melted into him. She hadn't given up on them.

All too soon, she pushed out of his embrace, leaving him with a hollow sensation at the pit of his stomach.

Her smile didn't bring a sparkle to her eyes as it normally did. "My mother sends her greetings."

He cleared his throat and flicked his gaze to the left. "I look forward to speaking to Her Royal Highness very soon." It wasn't a lie. He just hadn't mentioned the conversation they'd had the day he'd arrived in Bagumi.

She sat in the armchair facing the door, leaving him with the couch. Since when did she not want to sit close to him?

"My mother said she can help us to elope." She'd delivered the news as if she were reading an obituary.

He focused on the positive information rather than the tone that caused his stomach to contract. "That's great."

"She gave us a condition."

He ran a hand over his face and breathed out through his mouth. Conditions were never easy, but they'd manage. "What is it?"

Her throat bobbed with her gulp as she stared into her lap. "I know we haven't talked about this. I recently came to the conclusion that I'd be the one to move, even though it would be hard at first. I knew that as long as I had you in my life, everything would be okay."

She looked up at him. "My mother loves me very much, and she knows how difficult it was for me to be away from home for the time I studied in Switzerland. Of course, she's also being selfish with her request because she'd like me close and accessible. I'm the only one who enjoys shopping as much as she does." Her giggle sounded forced and did nothing to ease his apprehension. "The only way she'll help us if you promise to move to Bagumi."

The anvil fell into his stomach. Had he heard correctly? Move to Bagumi? What about his family and friends? The practice he'd just opened? The US lifestyle he loved?

She reached for his hands. "You don't have to decide now. She gave us—well, you—a few hours before we have to give her a decision."

The tears in her eyes reflected in the wobble of her voice.

There was nothing he could say at that moment to ease the pain shining from her eyes. He was suffering his own. All he had ever known was life in Vermont. Before travelling to Bagumi, purely to visit Amira, he'd only been on vacation in New Zealand and Mexico, and even then, he'd gotten homesick. He doubted he'd be able to live anywhere other than the US. Would their love be enough to sustain him through a life of being away from everything he knew?

He didn't miss the disappointing irony of how he'd thought so when she would've had to make the sacrifice. Now, he wasn't sure.

He released her hands and stood. He reached the kitchen in only a few long strides as he plunged the fingers of both hands through his hair. His heart pounded as if he'd sprinted a full mile in the few back and forth rounds he did of the suite.

Swiping a hand over his face, he held a cupped palm over his nose and sucked in air. Finally, his mind cleared, and reason returned. He dropped his hands to his side and turned to see her watching him, her expression neutral.

Another wave of anxiety threatened to knock him over. He could always read her. He rushed to her side so they were back to eye level.

"Can't I talk to your mother? Tell her about my new practice and the expansion we're working on? We've started looking for places. By the time we're done growing, all of Vermont, hell, the Northeast, will be coming to one of our offices."

He massaged the back of his neck in an attempt to ease the tension. His dreams would crumble if he moved to Bagumi. "Can't I at least try to convince your mother to help us, and still let us move to the US?"

For the first time while they were in private, she gave off what he could only interpret to be the cool aura of a royal. Not as powerful as her mother, but still potent. At that moment, he knew he'd lost her.

"I understand how very difficult it is to leave a place you have always called home." She crossed her legs at the ankles and perched her clasped hands on her lap. "It was highly presumptuous of my mother to request such an impossible task. Bagumi possesses all the comforts of home, yet it is not your home. I truly understand."

Who was this severely formal woman seated before him? He'd rather have her upset or scowling, telling him to wise up rather than behave as if they were strangers. "Amira, the news came as a shock I—"

She held up a hand and tilted her head to the right. He could almost see a tiara. "Your distressed actions of just a few moments ago revealed your thoughts rather clearly. I am sorry to have caused you angst on your visit to Bagumi. Unfortunately, I will not be able to act as your guide as initially planned. For this, I apologize. I will get a suitable escort for both you and Calvin so you can continue to experience the extraordinary beauty of the land."

She stood and slid her hands down her skirt before graceful steps led her to the door.

He scrambled to reach her when his brain activated his feet to function. He grasped her arm. She looked down at where they joined and glanced up at him. Her lips thinned, eyes squinted, and smoke virtually came out of her nostrils as they flared.

He released her with haste.

"Amira, we need to talk about this. I love you and want to be with you, but you can't just throw this life-altering decision at me and expect me to accept it without question. This is a change in my career and my whole existence we're talking about. It doesn't just affect me, but my family and business partners, as well. It isn't something to be taken lightly or decided at a moment's notice."

He put his hands behind his back to keep from touching her again. She had to listen to reason. The woman he'd gotten to know held little resemblance to this stranger staring at him unblinking.

She nodded. "I have assessed over the years that how a person reacts is how they really feel about a matter. Overthinking and rationalizing the situation may make you change your mind, but that initial thought, that primary thought, is your truth. I will accept and respect it. You should, too."

He clenched his jaw as she slipped further away from him while standing in the same spot. "I've heard that similar nonsense, too. I swear it isn't true, not for me. Fear of the unknown caused me to react that way. Can't we sit down and discuss this? Please, Amira."

For a moment, the woman he knew flashed into her eyes as the aloofness rescinded and a frown appeared. She reached behind her neck. When she brought her hands forward, she dragged the chain of her necklace upward. The gold strand was looped inside of the engagement ring he'd given her.

He backed away as the alarm bells went off in his head. He had to do something before she returned it. To convince her to talk. To listen. He shook his head, refusing to accept that they were over, because they weren't.

"We can work it out." His voice came out higher, and he cleared his throat. "There's nothing we can't get through, together. Just give us a chance. Everything will work out. I promise. We just need to discuss it. It's what our relationship is based on. Communication."

Amira obviously didn't believe so. Rather than chase him, she removed the ring from the chain and placed it on the side table near the couch. The sad, sweet smile she gave him made his heart clench so tightly that he clamped a hand over the area to protect it.

"It has been my greatest pleasure getting to know you, Jacob Pettersen. I wish you the absolute best in life."

The words flipped the switch from desperation to anger, and he said the first thing that came to mind he knew would snap her out of the robotic state she'd plunged herself into. "You aren't behaving like the mature woman I thought you were. No wonder your family still treats you like the baby of the family. I'm sure that once you start acting like an adult, they'll treat you like one."

For a moment, her eyes flashed up at him.

He cut her off before she could open her mouth to speak. "Adults discuss important issues, not rely on bogus theories to determine a person's behaviour." He took a breath and released it in a hard puff. "Did you really expect me to get on the phone to my mother, who also misses me when I'm away, and tell her that I was moving to Bagumi forever the moment you gave me the ultimatum? That's not the way it works, Princess. At least, not in the real world. You don't snap your fingers and then have people do your bidding."

"Is that how you see me Jake?" Her voice came out just as harsh as his, and yet, they'd both refrained from yelling. "As a spoilt princess who always has to have her way?"

"It wasn't until this moment, but now, my eyes seem to have seen the truth of who you really are. I don't think we're as good a match as we thought." He pointed to his chest and shook his head. "This pauper would never be able to tolerate not being seen as an equal in your eyes. Just someone to order about and obey. No."

His chest rose and fell with the heaviness of his breaths as they faced off in a stare down. At least now, that fire had returned to her.

He claimed victory when she looked away first. Were those tears in her eyes?

She turned, opened the door, and left.

Body trembling, her absence finally registered, and he ran to the door and flung it open.

What had he done? He hadn't meant it. Not the way it had come out in the heat of the moment.

A frantic search to the right and then the left found the hallway completely empty. He sprinted along the marble floors in search of her. Nothing. Heading in the opposite direction, he prayed to spot her.

Gone.

In her home, she wouldn't be found unless she wanted to be.

He'd lost the woman he'd sworn he'd do anything for.

CHAPTER NINETEEN

Amira had let go of the man she'd wanted to spend the rest of her life with. Released him like the proverbial butterfly who needed to fly free. Why didn't that same proverb share just how hard it would be to know that she'd live without the man she knew she belonged with?

When she had walked into his suite, she hadn't been sure if she'd be able to do it, but one look at how her mother's request had affected him and she couldn't let him go through with it.

A marriage brought on under a time of duress was no way to start a life together. She wouldn't shackle him to her problems. She cared about him too much.

His words had cut. He'd used just the right ones to cause her a lot of pain. That's how well he knew her. She would've thought his intentional cruelty might have made it easier to leave him.

It hadn't.

She had admired him for his courage at standing up to her when she'd clearly been wrong. She had acted immature. She'd done it for his sake, but he'd never know because they wouldn't see each other again.

She'd done the right thing.

Why did the fact that he never raised his voice at her, even when the veins had been popping out from the sides of his neck with anger, make her doubt her decision?

If they'd been able to stay together and had gotten married, he would have treated her with respect and kindness, like a true gentleman, even when under stress or irate like he'd been.

She'd run straight to her mother's quarters after the horrible ordeal and told her everything. From Jake's initial reaction to how she'd broken up with him because she couldn't stand to see him so tormented about leaving the only home he'd ever known.

The queen had smiled when she'd mentioned how he'd called her out on her behaviour. And how he'd basically agreed with her on being a spoilt princess.

Then, her mother had done what she'd least expected and told her pack her things.

***

Repeated calls to Amira had been met with a computerized voice telling him that the phone had been switched off, which sounded a lot like *go to Hell*.

When Jake had called Zareb to ask if he knew of Amira's whereabouts, all he'd gotten was a growl before the click had hit his ear. When he'd called back, the phone had kept ringing. Either Amira was right and the man was psychic, or she'd given him the rundown of what had happened as soon as she'd left him.

Their conversation replayed a dozen times.

How could someone spring something so major on a person and not expect hesitation? Life consisted of well-thought-out decisions. Spontaneity led to regrets, something he hated.

He'd come to her ready to commit. The ring should've proved it to her. She should've understood that the decision her mother had attempted to force on him needed to be discussed. He would have chosen her in the end because he'd done so long before his arrival.

He'd wanted her in his life, and now, she was gone because he...

Hell, he didn't know what he'd done wrong except for being honest. Could he have not agreed with her comment about being a spoiled princess? Definitely. But the shock he'd experienced at the bomb she'd dropped couldn't have been helped.

After all, he was a normal human being and had the right to not be in control every moment of his life, just as long as he made rational decisions after the fact.

Now, he was ready to fix the mess so they could be together again. He just had to find her first.

Taking a walking tour with a guard through the palace had yielded nothing. Not even his escort would tell him the location of Amira's apartment, or where she'd hidden herself. The single moment of hesitation had driven her away. Had he truly lost her?

Jake didn't need Calvin repeatedly telling him that he'd been an ass to figure it out.

His business partners would be affected by the abrupt move. It would mean a major disruption or even an end to their practice, and yet, Calvin had reprimanded him. Not being able to hear her sweet voice had had him lying awake all night, thinking about how to get her back. An unrelenting pressure squeezed his heart. He could barely tolerate the pain of not having her in his life for one day. He couldn't imagine how miserable a lifetime without her would be.

Being with Amira was most important. He'd start a new practice and prosper with her at his side.

He woke up his parents at midnight, their time, and broke the news about his move to Bagumi to be with the woman he loved. After all the times he'd spoken about her, they weren't surprised at the decision. They'd always wanted the best for him and

147

knew he wouldn't make a decision that didn't serve him.

The queen wouldn't be up for visitors at four in the morning. He'd have to wait until a decent hour to schedule an audience with her. She'd been willing to help them elope. Hopefully, she still was.

Other than through Amira, he only had access to the queen through the men who protected their little sister as if she were the most precious person in the world. Which she definitely was. At least to him.

Jake spent the early morning hours thinking about what he'd say to Zawadi that would make him listen. When the pseudo-respectable time of seven o'clock hit, he left the room and headed towards Zawadi's office. He'd wait until the man arrived. The prince set to be king had to help him.

Just as he'd paced the area for the hundredth time in fifteen minutes, he turned to come face to face with the last person he'd wanted to see. "Good morning."

"What are you doing in front of my brother's office?"

The question would've made more sense if Jake had been the one to ask it of Zareb. Did the man have no life? He stood to his full height and looked the head of security in the eyes. "I'm waiting for Za—"

"Prince."

Jake's jaw clenched at the removal of the title-free basis they'd originally been on. The man wasn't going to make things easy for him. "Pardon me. For Prince Zawadi to arrive so I can speak to him."

"If it's about Amira, he won't entertain you."

Jake tightened his fists in frustration. He had no reason to believe Zareb was lying. Hadn't Amira said that he never did? He had one last chance to find the woman he loved, and he'd take it, through humility. "I didn't mean to hurt Amira. She sprang the information about my having relocate to Bagumi so quickly that fear had me reacting."

When Zareb didn't pivot and walk in the opposite direction, he continued. "I'm in love with your sister. I wouldn't have come here with an engagement ring willing to marry her if I didn't want to be with her. Life in Vermont is all I've ever known. Like any other person faced with such a severe and sudden change, I panicked. To be honest, she blindsided me."

Zareb crossed his arms over his chest and widened his stance. "Why didn't you tell her this?"

"I tried. I wanted to discuss it with her, but she shut down when she saw the uncertainty in my initial reaction. She refused to talk about it. The next thing I knew, she'd shocked me even further by taking off my ring. That's when the anger kicked in and we had a disagreement, which was much better than her refusal to talk."

He held his arms out, exposing himself along with his greatest mistake. "She'd put the ring on the side table and left by the time my stunned brain sent the message to get my ass moving. By then, she'd disappeared."

To his horror, a smile came to Zareb's lips. "I have the most impatient, stubborn, entitled sister in the world."

Jake's back shot up straight, ready to defend his woman. "She's not that bad. I disappointed her. I just wish we could've discussed it. She would've seen that my initial reaction doesn't reflect the decision that's in my heart."

Zareb relaxed his arms at his sides. "Which is?"

"I'd move to Antarctica to be with her if she asked. Living with her in this paradise will be Heaven on Earth."

"What about your career?"

"The people in Bagumi have teeth. I've seen some of them. I'm sure I can register and start a practice here and thrive. Eventually. All I know is that I don't want to be without Amira."

Jake refused to flinch as Zareb stared at him.

"What were you going to discuss with my brother?"

An easy question.

"I wanted to speak with the queen." He glanced around and lowered his voice. "She said she'd help Amira and me to elope. I need to explain what happened between us to see if she's still willing to help."

"And if Amira no longer wants you?"

His abdominal muscles flexed as if he'd been punched just as invisible hands clenched around his throat. "I have to try to convince her of how much I love her. That I want only her for the rest of my life."

Did he believe him? Another lengthy silence set the hairs at the back of his neck to standing. Zareb turned and walked a few feet down the hallway.

When Jake didn't move, he glanced over his shoulder. "You can't win my sister back by standing around like a love-sick fool."

Jake's legs became gelatinous with relief as he realized that Zareb would help him by introducing him to the queen. He jogged to Zareb's side. "Thank you."

"I'm not the only one you need to convince of your sincerity and intentions. The woman you need to encounter has the strength of will of five hundred men. And yet, her heart is larger than the world."

Zareb seemed to have the greatest respect for his mother. Jake gulped at the thought of meeting Queen Zulekha. Again.

After an interminable walk down the marbled hallway, Zareb pointed towards the guest wing once they'd reached the front entrance. "Go to your room and pack your things. Tell Calvin to do the same."

Having expected to be led to the queen, Jake was thrown by the order. Was the man kicking him out of the country? He bent his arms at the elbows and flipped his palms upward as he'd seen Amira do when questioning something he'd done. "What's going on? Why do I have to pack?"

"I'm taking you to the queen as you would've requested of Zawadi. She's travelled to her homeland of Onsa where her brother sits as king.

Dread seeped into him at the thought of meeting even more royalty, but he attempted to appear stoic by lifting his chin and squaring his shoulders. One day, he'd learn to not reveal his emotions like Zareb had mastered. "Thank you. Where should we meet you when we're ready?"

Zareb's eyes glittered. Was the man impressed? He shouldn't be. Jake was on a mission to get Amira back, and he'd make it happen no matter how rough things got.

"I need to get some things settled. I'll meet you at your room in an hour."

Leaving in five minutes would've made him happier. "Can I say goodbye to Amira before we go?"

The response was quick and final. "No."

Zareb dismissed him by walking away.

Hope. Something he didn't have last night now warmed limbs which had been cold. If he could get the queen on his side, then Amira would be sure to listen to him. Once it happened, he'd convince her that the only place they needed to be was with each other.

CHAPTER TWENTY

Over thirty-six hours had trudged by since the possibility of being happy with Jake had been shot dead. The fact that she'd been the one to end it made it hurt even more.

Would he have given up everything he knew in order to fulfil the chance to be with her? She'd never know. It really hadn't been fair that she'd had to force the decision on him and had recanted it along with their relationship.

He'd find someone to be with that wouldn't embroil him in political mayhem. Someone he wouldn't have to save or change his entire life for just because he had a protective nature. She wouldn't abuse it.

They'd been perfect on every level. Her core throbbed as she remembered just how deliciously compatible they'd been physically. He'd incited her passion, leaving her longing for more even while satiated.

She released a sigh. Something she couldn't seem to stop doing since she'd forced her tears to abate. At least, the puffiness in her eyes had reduced. And yet, the emptiness gutting her couldn't be filled. Her mother had doted on her. Even her uncle, the king of Onsa, had attempted to cheer her. She'd summoned a smile for him, but couldn't enjoy his company as much as she normally did.

"It is good to be home," her mother said as they walked through the palace.

It wasn't as sprawling or extravagant as her father's palatial estate, but it was beautiful.

Amira turned a sharp gaze to her mother, not believing what she'd heard. "But your home is Bagumi."

"It is possible to have more than one, is it not?" She waved her hands in a graceful motion indicating her environment. "I grew up here. For the first eighteen years of my life, it was all I knew, and I was unconditionally loved. This is something you can never let go of."

So why had her mother expected it so readily of Jake?

For the first time since she'd left him, logic overruled emotion. Placing a hand over her eyes, she groaned. Her mother had loved her childhood home but had left it to be with her father.

Why hadn't she given him a chance to think about it and decide for himself instead of stealing the option away from him by ending their relationship? Maybe he would've chosen to stay with her in Bagumi, maybe not. Her abject stubbornness had stolen the choice from him.

"What's wrong, Amira?"

Looking back on their conversations, her mother had been hinting at the thing that had just slapped her first on the left and then the right cheek. "I never gave Jake the chance to make a decision."

He mother's brows rose to almost touch the rim of her head-tie. She grabbed Amira's hand and pulled her into a room and settled them down on the couch. "Finally, her eyes are open."

"Mama!"

"They are. You stole that boy's chance to be a hero in your eyes. To forgo everything to move to Bagumi."

"What if he'd chosen not to stay?"

154

Her mother waved down a hand. "Then he could sit in his coach airline seats and never look back, for all I care. It would have shown his true character of being a man of words rather than one of action. Proof of their devotion is always what we want."

She slid her finger along a crease in her skirt, avoiding her mother's dark eyes. "Of course, I hadn't expected him to jump up and down with excitement when I told him about your offer, but he'd been so agitated." She swung a finger from side to side. "Pacing up and down for the longest time. I thought he'd tear out his beautiful hair before the conversation was over." She raised heavy shoulders and let them fall as the weight of her rash decision weighed on her. "I took pity on him and opted out so he wouldn't be so distressed.

Her mother laughed. "Oh, my daughter. When are you going to stop being impetuous? It always gets the better of you."

Amira didn't join in the laughter. This time, her mistake had cost her the love of her life.

"Ever since you were small, you've been my most mischievous child. I don't know if you felt the need to compete with your older brothers or to ensure that I acquired my grey hairs early." She laughed as she touched her impeccably styled updo flowing from the head-tie.

"Since you went away for school, you've become more level-headed. Shall I say less obstinate in your views? As if you're now willing to look at more than what you know or personally want out of the situation.

"I attributed it to you living on your own, distanced from the comfort of your family. When you first told me about your *friend* Jake months ago, I knew the true reason for the transition. You're an extraordinary woman, but he brings out a calm within you that you didn't have before. This is why I allowed Zawadi to have him come to the palace."

Amira's eyes rounded.

"Yes, it was me. I know everything that happens in my home."

"You sound like Zareb."

Her mother's eyes gleamed with her wink. "Where do you think he acquired the skill? I've known about your relationship basically the whole time. I needed to assess him personally. When we spoke in private on the day of his arrival to the palace—"

Amira held up both hands, waving them high and wide like sports referees tended to. Had she just heard correctly? "What? When? He never told me."

"I told him not to. Another plus in his favour that he listened to instructions. By the way, you aren't the only sneaky royal in the palace." Slight wrinkles appeared at the corners of her stunning mother's eyes as she smiled.

"Why do you think you were mandated to continue working on that day? Don't worry, I was the quintessential queen during our meeting, putting extra force behind my haughty voice. He didn't cower as he answered the questions with directness, honesty, and respect. I knew he was right for you when he answered the question that cut the interview short."

Fear and curiosity warred. "What did you ask him?"

"I asked him if he would be okay playing second fiddle by getting into a relationship with you."

Amira slapped her palm over her eyes. "Oh my goodness, Mama! Why would you ask such a thing?"

She peeked out through her fingers. "What did he say?"

"We are royalty, Amira. No matter where we go in the world, we get noticed whether people know us or not. Jake wasn't born into our world. He's special in his own way, but he's never been adored by people who would literally let us walk over them so we don't get ourselves dirty. We were born to shine and we do it exceedingly well.

"Unless our mates are born of the same ilk, they will lag behind. Perhaps in many years, they will catch up, but it will be a knock to his ego to be in the background whenever you are together in public. No matter if you're here or in the US."

Amira couldn't argue against something she'd experienced all of her life. The only time all eyes in a room didn't turn to her was when she was with her family. Even then, people clamoured for her attention.

"How did he respond?"

Her mother's smiled made her appear younger. "That even if you weren't a princess, you'd always be first with him and would expect others to treat you the same way."

She slid her hand to her chest and flung back into the couch at his bone-melting sweetness. And then, she jumped to her feet with the realization that she'd tossed him away. Doing it because she'd thought it was for his own benefit didn't make her less jittery with the need to get him back. Or had it been to keep him from stomping on her pride with a negative answer?

"Mama, I have to fly to Bagumi right now to see him. I've made a horrible mistake. I took the coward's way out by not waiting to possibly be rejected." She flung her shoulders back. "That's not something you taught us. I need to rectify things by letting him make up his own mind."

Her mother smiled and patted the seat next to her. "Sit down."

Fighting the urge to sprint from the room so she could head back, she lowered herself.

"You have become a woman that I am extremely proud to call my daughter."

Amira's racing heart calmed at her mother's touching words. "It's because I've had the best mother in the world."

The queen dipped her chin with her eyes slightly hooded. "Quite right."

Their similar giggles filled the room.

"The whole situation with Duak and the engagement was an unfortunate occurrence," her mother said. "If your father had come to me for advice as he normally does, I would've guided him in another direction." She brushed strands of Amira's dreads over her shoulder. "What are you going to do about Jake when you see him again?"

"Apologize until I'm blue in the face and then do it some more. If he doesn't want to move to Bagumi to be with me, then I'll respect his decision. Maybe we can find another way to be together."

"It's always best to follow your heart and communicate. Whatever happens, make sure to listen to him."

"I will. Thank you, Mama."

Her mother leaned over and kissed her forehead. "You are always my pleasure. How about putting some make-up on and getting dressed in something less frumpy?"

"You've been wanting to tell me that all day, haven't you?"

Her mother stood. "Don't worry about going back to Bagumi. I have everything taken care of."

Amira stared at her, attempting to figure her out. A fruitless venture. "What have you done?"

"Go change. You'll find out soon enough."

CHAPTER TWENTY-ONE

Jake caught the vase before it could crash to the floor. He'd hate to imagine how much he'd have to pay for the antique-looking piece if his reflexes hadn't been so quick.

He proceeded to pace the room without getting near anything he could knock over.

"You need to sit down," Zareb said as they waited for his mother to arrive.

Rather than heeding the advice, he went to the window. The far-reaching manicured lawn led to a bridge over the water that they'd had to cross. This palace seemed more like a fortress than the one in Bagumi. Zareb had explained that the monarchs on his mother's side used to have a penchant for war and needed the protection.

The door opened, and he swung around. His heart twisted as reverence filled a single whispered word. "Amira."

The feeling of déjà vu hit him as they stared at each other, both open-mouthed. He took an involuntary step in her direction as she did the same.

"Good afternoon, Jake."

He blinked and tore his attention from Amira to the queen. When had she entered? He walked in her direction, placed his hands so they touched his back with his elbows extending out, and bent at the waist while keeping his eyes downcast.

"I see someone had been teaching you our ways."

He stole a glance at Amira. "Yes, Your Royal Highness."

"I am happy to see it. Come, Zareb. We will leave them to speak alone."

When the two left the room, the tension multiplied. He looked directly at the most beautiful woman he'd ever met, and his skin tingled.

"I'm sorry."

Her voice had come out clearly, but he questioned his hearing.

He tapped his fingers on his chest. "*I'm* sorry. All I want is to be with you. I shouldn't have hesitated about moving."

She rushed towards him. "I didn't think it was fair to stress you out with such a huge decision, especially since it was just to get me out of a bind, so I rescinded it by breaking things off."

She held up a hand when he opened his mouth to speak. "I wasn't completely altruistic in my motives, though. I may have been terrified that you'd say no. I'm sorry I didn't give you the chance to make your own decision."

Relief tickled him, and he smiled. He reached out, grabbed her hands, and kissed the knuckles of each. "Amira, you're all I need. You're my everything. I'm willing to move anywhere you are because you're my world. Will you have me as your husband?"

Her smile sent his heart soaring.

"Yes, Jake. Yes!" she shouted as her feet did some kind of jig before she catapulted herself onto him.

He swung her around before settling her on her feet. Her kiss set his body on fire, and he wanted to find her bedroom to seal the proposal in a more intimate manner. He forced himself to release her, took out the ring she'd returned, and placed it on her finger.

"I promise not to try to let my stubbornness get the better of me," she murmured.

"And I vow to put you first."

She reached up and touched his cheek. "I can't believe I was so stupid to let you go. Don't think you will ever be able to shake me ever again."

He turned his head and kissed the palm of her hand. "I wouldn't want it any other way, my queen."

They stared into each other's eyes for the longest time as the strength of their emotions crackled through the room.

She cleared her throat. "How in the world did you get Zareb to bring you here? When I told him what had happened, he swore he'd find a way to make you suffer." She cringed as his skin blanched. "To be fair, I didn't tell him the part where I called it off before you could give me an answer. Just about how you'd reacted."

He nodded. "I was desperate for any chance to see you again. I think he liked that. When I went to Zawadi's office half past the crack of dawn so he could help me speak to your mother, Zareb met me there instead. I told him what had happened and how I'd been in the wrong."

"I love you so much, Jake. You are my brave knight and king all rolled into one because attempting to request an audience with my mother took guts."

"I love you, Amira."

Before he could taste her lips, the door opened, and Zareb appeared. "Mother told me to escort you to see Uncle Machie."

Jake's brows crinkled together. He'd been introduced to the king of Onsa when he'd first arrived. Why were they being escorted to him again?

Amira didn't seem to find it strange as she stood on her toes and kissed him on the cheek, retrieving his attention. It had to be the sweetest one he'd ever had.

He knew he'd never regret moving to Bagumi to be with this incredible woman.

Amira couldn't feel her feet touch the floor as they walked into her uncle's office. Her brothers tended to joke and call it the war room. Uncle Machie had taken on his ancestor's militant ways and kept his army of citizens prepared and ready. No country ever dared make trouble with the Kingdom of Onsa.

The room contained few people. Her mother stood at the left-hand side of Uncle Machie while his wife stood on the right. Calvin had found a spot next to one of her female cousins. Why were they standing like that? She'd never seen a formation like this before.

Amira and Jake bowed before the king in unison and stood waiting to hear his command.

"Your mother tells me that you wish to be married to this man. Is this correct?"

She swung her gaze to her mother. The queen's neutral expression gave nothing away. What was going on? She recovered within seconds. "Yes, Uncle."

He averted his attention to Jake. "And do you wish to marry my niece?"

Jake looked him in the eyes with his head partly lowered. "Yes, Your Majesty."

Impressed at his deference, she almost clapped as her confusion was replaced with pride.

"You are willing to go against your father's decree and pay the consequences in order to see it happen."

Jake and Amira looked at each other as understanding shone on her. If his lop-sided grin was any indicator, he'd also gained clarity.

They spoke in unison as if they'd rehearsed. "We are."

Uncle Machie's smile was sudden and broad. "So am I. Come closer."

Amira couldn't hold back her giggle. Her uncle, although he liked her father, would intentionally come up with ways to irritate the man. He called his prerogative for stealing his sister away years ago. To his credit, her father played along. The king would never admit it, but Amira sensed his fear of her militant uncle.

Her father would never challenge her uncle's decision to allow them to marry. Never.

Her uncle stretched out his left hand. Zareb, who had taken his place next to her mother, placed a small box in it. Calvin placed a similar container in the palm of the king's right hand.

"As the absolute monarch of Onsa, I have had the privilege of officiating many weddings. Nothing gives me greater pleasure than yours, Amira and Jake. You have already stated that you wish to marry each other. If you are willing to do so right this moment, then each of you should take the box closest to you and open it."

They were actually getting married right then and there? She held back a celebratory dance as greed and anticipation drove her to snatch hers while Jake's retrieval came with more calm.

It took her a moment to clear her haze of joy and focus on the gold band glittering up at her from inside of her box.

"Turn to each other. Amira Oware Saene, read what is inscribed in the ring," her uncle said.

"Forever One."

She couldn't keep the tears banked, and if she wasn't mistaken, Jake's eyes glistened with his own.

"Jacob Russell Pettersen, read what is inscribed in your ring."

He cleared his throat, looked at the gold band, and smiled at her. "One Forever."

"The same words in reverse order, meaning the same thing. Nothing but death will ever break this union. Whatever trials, tribulations, or joyous events may come your way, you will weather it. Together. As one. You will be to each everything the other needs. You will love each other as you love yourself, because you are one forever, and forever one." He paused to let the words sink in.

"Jacob, place the ring on Amira's finger." Uncle Machie waited until the cool, elegant metal glittered against her skin.

"Amira, place the ring on Jake's finger."

She did as instructed and returned the smile of the man her heart had chosen.

"Join hands."

Uncle Machie placed his right hand over theirs. And then, he invited the others to do the same. "You are witnesses that what has been joined this day will never be broken. They are to walk in this world together, forever."

"Forever," Amira mouthed.

"Forever," Jake said.

"You are now married in the sight of God, your family, and the law. Congratulations."

The ceremony didn't end with a kiss; the smiles of complete adoration she both gave and received would do. She'd have the rest of her life to attempt to get her fill of Jake. She had a feeling she never would.

CHAPTER TWENTY-TWO

Still on a high from the surprise wedding, Amira pinched the underside of her arm to make sure it had all been real. The pain verified it. So did the rings glimmering on her finger. She couldn't forget her two-hour-old husband smiling so hard at her from across the room that she doubted he could see from the slits of his eyes.

The family had celebrated after the ceremony with food, wine, and a lot of laughter.

Although ecstatic to have married Jake, she wished her whole family and friends could've borne witness to the ceremony. She missed her father and the fact that he hadn't walked her down the aisle like she'd always imagined would happen.

The disappointing thought must have registered on her face because her mother placed a hand on her shoulder. "What's wrong, Amira?"

"I wish Baba and the others could have been here." She still hadn't gotten over the fact that her father had chosen Bagumi over her. Yet, her love for him still prevailed.

Her mother's dark-eyed gaze steadied on her. "Some things cannot be, but we will celebrate when we return home."

"I've disobeyed him. I don't think I'll be welcome."

The older woman's laughter drew the attention of those close to them. "You have so much to learn, my daughter."

Indignant about the slight, she frowned.

"There's no one in all of West Africa—" she extended her arms out wide, "—dare I say the whole continent, who would dare go against the Onsa. The fear and respect for my kinsmen flows too deeply. Since my brother has performed the ceremony, your father has no other choice than to accept it."

Amira's brows creased together. "But what about King Lahib of the Ashani? Won't he think Baba deceived him?"

"He will understand because your father didn't know of it. He wasn't the one to break the betrothal. You were. They have nothing to blame Bagumi for, except your stubbornness in refusing to be forced into a marriage you didn't desire."

She nodded, unable to stop smiling. "I'll be happy to take the blame."

"Good. Don't worry about your father. He may have to dole out consequences for your insubordination, but he would never cast you out of your home. He cares for you too greatly to lose the light you bring to our family.

Amira wound her arms around her mother. "I love you, Mama."

"I love you, my daughter."

She sniffled and basked in her mother's embrace before the older woman pulled away.

"I know you don't need advice of a sexual nature—"

"Mama!"

Could her face flame anymore? At twelve, she'd wanted to run out of the room screaming when her mother had sat her down for the sex talk. The times they'd spoken about sex later on had been easier to bear, if not still a bit uncomfortable. When she'd lost her virginity at nineteen, she'd confided in her mother, who had been more concerned about her having protected herself than anything else.

"— but just make sure that you consummate the marriage tonight before we leave for Bagumi tomorrow. It will ensure that you belong to each other. I have made arrangements for you to sleep in the same room and have placed an array of lingerie in your bag."

Amira's head definitely needed dousing with some ice water before she set the place on fire. "Thank you."

The queen of mortifying her daughter held up a finger. "And one last thing. Remember to treat each other as if it were the last day you'll ever speak again. My mother told me this. I have lived it and held it in my heart for just this moment. Treat what you have as precious, because it is."

Her mother didn't have to tell her twice. She'd take the advice to heart.

Jake came to them and wrapped an arm around her shoulders. "I missed you."

The room disappeared as she gazed into dark sapphire blue eyes.

The clearing of her mother's throat brought them back to reality. "Before I leave you two alone, I need to tell you that you are no longer forced to live in Bagumi."

Amira's eyes went wide. After all the trouble the promise had brought them, she was relinquishing it?

Her mother held up a solitary hand and waved it.

"You always said that you would not test your man as tends to be tradition. I disagreed with you and did it on your behalf. Now you know just how far Jake is willing to go for you." As if her mother had done them a favour, she graced them with a wide smile. "You two may decide where you would like to live. My preference is Bagumi, but then again, I'm the queen of the magnificent country, and am completely biased."

She walked away with a tinkle of laughter in her wake.

"Your mother is amazing."

Amira turned to him with her mouth gaping. "You still think so after the rift she helped to create between us?"

A lock of his light brown hair slipped onto his forehead. She reached up and smoothed back the silky strands. She'd have no difficulty getting used to touching him more frequently.

"She was looking out for your best interest." His hand slipped to her waist and pinched, making her giggle and jump. "Besides, how could I be angry at a woman who paved the way towards allowing me to marry you? She's brilliant, and no one can tell me otherwise."

"Hmmm." Amira didn't hold the same positive view about her mother's meddling, but in their case, the ends had justified the means. "We still need to decide where we're going to live."

"Not tonight, we don't. Your mother told me we had to consummate the marriage in order to make it unbreakable." His left eyelid lowered in a wink. "That's my main focus."

"She didn't!" The room became much too warm as her skin flushed with embarrassment. "What did you say?"

"Yes, Your Majesty."

Amira laughed as she took his hand, leading them to the door. "She told me the same thing. I think it's time to obey the queen's order. What do you think?"

His long strides outmatched hers until he tugged her along. "I say, long live the queen."

CHAPTER TWENTY-THREE

Not for the first time, Amira stopped herself from gnawing on her nails by crossing her arms over her chest.

"It's going to be okay," Jake leaned in and whispered. "Your father loves you."

Her ears perked up at the sound of footfalls. Duak and his brother strode down the hallway to where she and Jake waited for an audience with her father. A tremor of anger ran through her at Duak's snarl of hostility when she turned and met his eyes. He must've gotten the message that she and Jake had married. Good.

Controlling the situation, she smiled in the face of his animosity before breaking eye contact and rested a hand on her husband's arm.

"Duak isn't happy with us," she sing-sang.

Jake's lips paled as they formed a thin line. He stared at the prince. "That's too damn bad."

The door to her father's office opened, and they were invited in by the receptionist. They entered and bowed. When the receptionist left, her father indicated that they should sit in the four seats presented before his desk.

Her fear came back in full force as she sat before the commanding presence of her father. She forced herself not to squirm as he glowered at her for several seconds.

"Amira, you have broken the betrothal and married against my decree and without my knowledge."

Was he expecting an answer with his pause, or just letting the news sink into the room? He sounded more resigned to the fact than angry. That had to be a good sign.

He continued as she was about to speak.

"Due to your actions, the marriage contract between Bagumi and Ashani has been obliterated." He looked at each person in the room in turn, keeping his gaze settled on Duak. "After discussing the matter with king of Ashani, we have come to the agreement that for the best interest of our people, peace will prevail between the two countries despite no unification of the monarchs through marriage."

Clapping and hooting seemed to be in order, but she refrained. A grunt of dissatisfaction came from Duak.

"Since you have blatantly disobeyed the throne, Amira, you must pay the consequences."

When Jake tipped his body forward as if getting ready to speak, she touched the back of her fingers against his outer thigh. No need to acquire more trouble than they were already in.

Her father didn't appreciate interruptions, as evidenced by the steely glare he gave Duak when he murmured in the affirmative of her father's statement.

"As your punishment, you have been banned from Bagumi."

What? She hadn't heard correctly. She couldn't have. The blood draining from her head, leaving her feeling dizzy while her heart threatened to burst out of her chest, told her that she'd heard the news she'd dreaded.

In her peripheral vision, she saw Duak's lips lift in an ugly smirk. Her hand itched to slap it off his face.

174

How could her father banish her from the only home she'd ever known? She placed a hand over her stomach and willed it to settle. She would not vomit in front of the king. What would she do if she never saw her family again? Jake's warm hand in hers helped decrease the sharp plunge of pain.

"The punishment will take effect in one week."

She squeezed Jake's fingers. She had only seven days to spend with her family on the land she'd been raised. It wasn't enough time. The inclination to fall to her knees and plead for a reprieve came on strong. He'd probably punish her further if she did.

Her father wasn't finished. "The banishment will be upheld for four months after you have left Bagumi."

Had she been sniffling too loudly to hear him correctly? She held her breath as she waited for confirmation.

"After said time, you and your husband may be allowed back into Bagumi as your punishment will have been completed." The last, he stated with a twinkle in his eyes.

She squelched the instinct to jump up and hug her father and holding on tight. He truly did love her. She stayed seated and smiled like a face-painted clown. She'd have both Jake and the chance to return to her home.

Duak couldn't hold his tongue. "This is not a sufficient sentence for her treacherous behaviour."

"Need I remind you in whose presence you sit, *Prince* Duak?"

The hard tone had Amira sympathizing for a moment as she recalled its potent use on her when she'd been younger.

The chastisement was enough to have Duak lowering his gaze to the floor even as his lips remained pursed. His impotent frustration made her giddy inside. She covered her mouth to hide an irrepressible smile. Karma could be very pleasant at times.

"Amira and Jake, stay seated. The others may go."

Duak opened his mouth and then must've thought better about speaking because he clamped his lips shut. He stood and glowered at her with retribution in his eyes before storming out of the room.

The short respite of relief gave way as her stomach filled with dread. How disappointed was her father at her behaviour? Banishing her for a mere four months as the king didn't mean he approved of her actions as a father. Would he forgive her for excluding him from one of the most important days of her life?

The prominent man she'd loved and respected all her life stood and came around his desk. Standing in front of her, he opened his arms. She rushed into them and held tight, sniffling into his broad chest as she'd done so many times as a child.

"I'm sorry, Baba. It wasn't my intention to defy you." She pulled back and viewed her father through blurred vision. "Jake and I are meant to be together."

"No need to apologize, my daughter. Love sometimes comes unexpectedly and changes your world forever. I understand."

Was he referring to the woman he'd married after her mother, or had there been someone else who'd captured his heart? She tucked the questions away to ask him at a later, more emotionally stable date.

He kissed her temple and released her before turning to her husband, who'd gotten to his feet as soon as her father had stood. The hand her father held towards Jake was met with a clasp of palm against palm, before her father pulled him in for a brisk back-slapping hug. Just like she'd seen him give her brothers.

The stress of uncertainty left her body at her father's acceptance.

The men then stood face to face.

"You will take care of my daughter."

The force driving the words couldn't be mistaken.

"Yes, Your Majesty."

"Good. Queen Zulekha speaks highly of you. Four months is not long to live outside of the palace. In that time, you may decide where you two belong in this world." The corners of his eyes crinkled with his smile. "I'm partial to Bagumi, but you may decide otherwise. Follow the calling of your heart and soul, just as you did when you found each other, and all will be well."

She stepped back into his arms. "Thank you, Baba."

His wise words would come to fruition. With Jake as her present and her future, she'd be happy wherever they landed.

EPILOGUE

Amira raised her arms in homage to the sky. The heat in Bagumi made her sweat through her light linen dress. Unlike her husband, she revelled in it. She laughed at his fulfilled promise as he'd dashed into the air-conditioned vehicle to wait for her.

After spending a winter in Vermont trudging through more snow than she ever wanted to see again, she'd never take the glorious sun of her country for granted again. She'd missed her home and her family over the past six months, but the time away had been necessary.

Together, she and Jake had made a decision they were happy about. It had taken the time to sell Jake's house and settle his portion of the practice into Calvin's name. He would start a new practice in Bagumi while volunteering some of his time to help those less fortunate in the villages. Both her father and Calvin said they'd be more than happy to help those in need of dental care who couldn't afford it.

Instead of working for her family as she'd initially desired, she'd partner her husband with the business aspect of his practice.

The best part of the move was that it had been Jake's suggestion, and he was as excited as she was.

He cracked a window. "Amira, please don't make me come out and get you."

She laughed as she strode to the vehicle and slid in to be with her husband.

Forever.

Thank you for reading His Defiant Princess. Carry on reading to find out more about the next book in the Royal House of Saene series.

BLURB: His Inherited Princess by Empi Baryeh

India Saene, Princess of Bagumi, must enter a marriage alliance to save her kingdom from an economic crisis. Tragedy strikes when her husband of a few hours is killed in an accident on the way to their honeymoon. She recovers from a coma two weeks later to discover she has been inherited by her husband's younger   brother!

Sheikh Omar El Dansuri has never wanted to be king, nor does he desire a wife. However, when his older brother dies, he not only becomes the future king of Sudar, but he also inherits his brother's bride through an age-old tradition. Falling for the headstrong India is out of the question especially when evidence points to her as his brother's killer.

Neither India nor Omar wanted this marriage, but the passion that burns between them cannot be denied. When India's secret is revealed, will either of them survive the consequences?

CHAPTER ONE: HIS INHERITED PRINCESS

BY EMPI BARYEH

"I'm sorry, My Lady, but your husband...Prince Majid didn't make it."

Something is wrong with that sentence.

Princess India Saene couldn't figure out what, though. Her muddled thoughts made it difficult to piece anything together.

The wedding. It was the last thing she remembered. Her marriage to Majid marked the beginning of an alliance between her kingdom, Bagumi, and the Sahelian kingdom of Sudar. She'd only met her husband a month before their wedding, and although they weren't a love match, he'd been the perfect host, and she'd believed they could eventually grow to love each other.

"Where is he?" she asked.

Her tongue felt like a piece of parchment paper in her mouth, dry and tasteless...weighty. She barely managed to slit open her equally heavy eyelids before the bright lights above forced her to shut them again.

"Erm..."

Hesitation. She frowned, but before she could ask why, her mind produced another memory: she and Majid in a car—on their way to their honeymoon.

What did the woman mean by Prince Majid didn't make it? Was she alone at their honeymoon? Why would he not come with her? His coronation, scheduled for next week, gave them barely five days for this trip. Why would he miss even a day?

Perhaps something to do with his father, King Rafael, who had announced his abdication for medical reasons not too long ago. From the little she knew of Majid, she couldn't think of anything else that would cause him to abandon her without prior notice. A year ago, her father had suffered a mild heart attack, which had sparked debate about him handing over to her eldest brother. Luckily, he'd bounced back and had been cleared by the doctors to resume work full-time.

She'd understand if a situation with King Rafael had caused Majid to cut their honeymoon short. Or had he informed her, and she couldn't remember? Frustration mounted as her mind simply refused to yield to her demands for recollection.

"When is he returning?"

"My Lady, I don't have the authority to respond to that."

"What do you mean?"

She pried her eyes open again, blinking. Her mind drifted off as her surroundings became clearer. White ceiling, stark white walls, a constant beeping sound...*and that smell*. A woman's face came into focus; she wore a mask of concern.

Recognition poured into India's mind. "Salma?"

Her Sudari personal assistant smiled, relief taking over her features. "You recognised me. Thank God. They said you might not, which would be a bad sign."

"Where are we?"

"We're at the hospital."

"Hospital?" The beeping sound fit with this explanation, but why would she be in a hospital and not on her honeymoon? "When is Majid returning?"

At the look of discomfort on Salma's face, threads of worry wound tight around India's chest.

"Salma, would you please give me a moment with my wife?" a male voice spoke before she could express her concerns.

The voice vibrated through her, putting a kick in her chest and a sense of calm in her heart. Strange, she'd never realised how deep Majid's voice was. She remembered it as a gentle tenor, but he'd just spoken in a tone more bass than tenor, issuing words with the smoothness of a warm knife cutting through butter.

"Of course, Your Royal Highness," Salma said, curtseying.

India tried sitting up, and a sharp pain zinged through her head and body, causing her to wince and lie back down.

"No, My Lady," a third person said. A female who spoke with gentleness, belying an unmistakable authority in her delivery. "You mustn't move."

"How are you?"

Her husband's deep voice washed over her.

Yes, she could definitely grow to fall in love with that voice. He sounded so close. She turned slowly, meeting his dark brown stare.

Confusion made her blink. Twice. The face staring back at her wasn't Majid's.

"Omar?"

The deep, smooth-as-butter voice belonged to Omar?

The brothers had similar eyes but bore little resemblance beyond that. Majid carried his lean, six-foot frame with the grace of an athlete, whereas Omar stood at about five-eleven, his muscular body honed to perfection. Both had undergone military training, which probably explained their extremely fit physiques, but Omar oozed sexual charisma and a certain feral attractiveness that probably had countless woman falling at his feet.

Even she had experienced a moment of breathlessness when she'd met him briefly a month ago, but she'd known better than to put any stock in such a fleeting sensation, especially since their first meeting had also marked her betrothal to his brother.

Yet, for some inexplicable reason, her mind retrieved images of their first encounter. She and her father had been led into the room where King Rafael and Majid had been waiting. Soon after the introductions, a knock had sounded, and Omar had entered. His gaze had captured hers, and for several seconds, she'd forgotten to breathe. The same thing had happened only moments after when they'd been introduced and he'd taken her hand.

She pushed aside the thoughts, focusing on her present need for answers. What was Omar doing here? Had Majid sent him?

"Is she in a lot of pain, Doctor?" Omar asked, his gaze directed at someone on the other side of the bed.

"She shouldn't be in unbearable pain, Your Royal Highness. In fact, we've reduced the dosage of her pain medication."

"Why are they calling you Your Royal Highness?"

As she'd been made to understand, there were three formal styles used in addressing members of the royal family in Sudar. 'Majesty' for the king, 'Royal Highness' for the Queen and the heir apparent, and 'Highness' for everyone else.

"Wh—where's Majid?"

Her voice grated against her dry throat. Worry snaked up her spine. Something was wrong. She felt it in her bones.

Omar looked at her, and she found herself trapped in his gaze.

"How much do you remember?"

She frowned. "Remember?"

As if his rich voice had unlocked a door, it came to her all at once. She and Majid had been in the car, discussing the protocols to be observed for his coronation. Funny, since he'd apparently already broken one rule by travelling in the same car with her. She remembered the relief with which she'd latched on to the topic, glad to take her mind off how they'd approach their first night as husband and wife.

Then...

Bang!

It sounded like a gunshot or maybe a canon. The car careened to the left. Everything happened so fast. The driver swore, maintaining an iron grip on the steering wheel, but the car kept speeding.

"Watch out!" Majid yelled.

Screeching tires, then another *bang*! Something had hit them. She only remembered seeing headlights at the window before they were airborne. The car may have flipped over before crashing to the ground. Then, everything went black.

She shut her eyes as if it would somehow turn off the faucet of memories. Warmth engulfed her, and she realised Omar had taken her hand as he sat on the bed.

"You and Majid had an accident," he said softly.

"How's he?"

Dread clutched her gut, telling her she knew the answer. *Prince Majid didn't make it.*

"Majid fought bravely, but eventually succumbed to his injuries."

"No," she whispered, tears filling her eyes.

For several seconds, she hoped this was a nightmare. She'd wake up and find Majid lying by her side, and they'd laugh about this weird dream. Because if this wasn't happening in her head, then it meant Majid had died; she was a widow. What did it mean for the alliance between their two nations?

Her mind was in no position to process matters of such enormity. She refocused on what Omar had said.

One word stuck in her mind.

"Eventually? How long have I been here?"

"Two weeks," he answered. "Since you're awake now, you'll be coming home soon."

Coming home. Why did that sound off? She frowned as something else occurred.

"You called me your wife."

He stared at her for a long moment as though trying to decide whether to answer.

"In accordance with our tradition, I inherited my brother's widow."

"What?" She looked beyond him at Salma who nodded. "How could we be married if I've been here the past two weeks?"

"We observed the obligatory ten days of mourning, but after that, nothing stopped us from performing the widow inheritance rites."

Her heart pounded, fuelled by fury. "You can't marry me without my consent."

"I'm afraid the alliance between our kingdoms supersedes your consent. Or mine, for that matter. The only party who needed to be consulted was your king."

"My father agreed to this? Does he even know I'm in the hospital?"

He nodded. "Your parents and your brother, Azikiwe, arrived here the day after the accident. King

Ibrahim returned for the marriage ceremony, and I've kept your family updated on your progress."

She shook her head, unable to wrap her mind around his words. Had her father truly been a part of this?

"Sire," the other female, whom India deduced from the lab coat and stethoscope was the doctor, interrupted. "She needs rest."

Omar nodded, although his gaze remained on India.

He leaned in. Panic stole into her. Did he mean to kiss her? She couldn't allow him to do that as if any of what he'd said was okay with her. She'd committed herself to his brother, not to him. She willed herself to speak, or turn away, but his musky scent surrounded her, engulfed her senses, and her voice caught in her throat.

She held her breath as his lips touched her temple. A flame ignited from the spot, expanding over her as hot threads of pleasure and confusion, and for a moment, she forgot the pain in her body.

Pulling back, he stood. "Rest now, *ya jameel*. We'll talk soon."

In her battered state, her heart had no defence against his allure or the endearment—*my beautiful*—uttered with the ease of a man used to having women fall at his feet. She found the strength to look away, shamed to discover her response to him hadn't been as fleeting as she'd convinced herself.

"Can I have a private word with you, Doctor?" Omar said.

"Certainly, Sire."

India shut her eyes against Omar's retreating figure, the gesture releasing unshed tears. In the solace of her mind's eye, she sought to reject his declaration, reject him.

However, her mind veered off course, focusing on the heat from his kiss. Guilt slammed into her. Majid's kiss at their wedding had been sweet, but it hadn't packed the kind of heat Omar's lips had aroused.

What could it mean? She'd never been given to ephemeral emotions. Love and passion didn't have a place in marriages of alliance.

Her reaction to the kiss had to be nothing more than a result of her jumbled emotions, because falling for Omar had to be all kinds of wrong.

***

Several hours later, Prince Omar El Dansuri sat at the expansive mahogany desk that had become his following his brother's demise. Their father, King Rafael, had unofficially stepped down a few weeks ago owing to failing health, and Majid was to have succeeded him. The stipulation of marriage before ascension to the throne had led to the speedy conclusion of the treaty between Sudar and Bagumi, as well as the marriage between Majid and India barely a month after their first meeting.

His brother should have been the one sitting at this desk right now, carrying the weight of a troubled nation on his shoulders. Without preamble, fate had thrust this responsibility on him; a position he wouldn't have been eligible for just half a century ago when ascension to the throne had required full Sudari bloodlines. His mother had been the daughter of a paramount chief from Northern Ghana, but her royal lineage didn't matter to the purists, nor did the fact that he'd never met her. His mother had died in childbirth, and he'd been raised by Queen Azmera, Majid's biological mother, as her own.

The same purists now stood against many of his reforms aimed at turning the kingdom's economy around—in particular, his campaign for Sudar to join the African Union and allow foreign diplomatic missions in. There were also many who agreed with his thinking, but the traditionalists believed opening up Sudar would affect the culture and traditions negatively.

A big proponent of this theory was his own uncle Sheikh Latif, Emir of the semi-autonomous state of Umm Jafar, who was next in line until Omar produced an heir. Although Uncle Latif had shown unwavering support for King Rafael, and even for Majid, he didn't misuse any opportunity to comment about what he would do differently if he were king.

Omar, on the other hand, had never desired the throne of Sudar with all its encumbrances, never coveted anything due his brother as the heir.

Until he'd set eyes on India Saene.

He remembered it clearly—walking into this very room. They'd been sitting on the comfortable sofas where the king received his guests; his father and brother on one, and King Ibrahim Saene of Bagumi and his daughter, India, on the other.

The moment he'd entered, his gaze had collided with hers, and for five whole seconds, everything in him had stilled. He'd only been released from her ensnaring eyes when his father had spoken, introducing her as Majid's fiancée. A sharp jolt had rocked his chest, a stab of jealousy, for the first time, for something belonging to his brother.

He'd torn his eyes away, making a mental note to stay as far away from her as possible, because even with the knowledge of her being his future sister-in-law, he'd still been too aware of her almond-shaped eyes, her succulent-looking lips, and the rise and fall of her breasts.

He wished he could have dismissed it as a passing fancy, or a result of a self-imposed celibacy, but three months without action didn't quite qualify as abstinence. He'd gone longer without sex and hadn't reacted in such a primal way to the first female he'd set eyes on.

His awareness of her had grown when she'd spoken about protecting children and creating equal opportunities for women in the sub-region, especially where old mind-sets still existed. She'd been eloquent, her voice echoing with intelligence and passion. For one unguarded moment, his mind had led him on an excursion of forbidden thoughts, and he'd wondered if she exhibited similar passion in other areas.

Now, she was his.

Her look of disbelief when he'd given her the news of their marriage had haunted him all afternoon. Though she hadn't said it, he sensed she meant to fight against their union. He had a feeling, too, that he knew why. She'd been willing to sacrifice her happiness to the marriage alliance when she'd been somewhat a part of the process.

This time, actions had been taken without her knowledge, and while their two fathers were within their rights for going ahead with the inheritance rights, his crash course on India Saene told him she wouldn't see it that way. She would most certainly fight him on this the moment she could get out of the hospital bed.

Normally, his default position to the marriage would have been resistance; a self-professed non-conformist, he'd always gotten a kick from doing the unexpected—a characteristic that had earned him the moniker Royal Pain, but even that had been like a badge of honour to his young self.

The trouble-making Omar had disappeared the day Majid died, fundamentally altering his priorities and killing his inert need for owning the shock factor.

Even if this weren't the case, he couldn't pretend he didn't desire India. Now that she was his, he didn't plan on letting her go. He just needed to figure out how to win her heart before it was too late.

Taking a deep breath, he returned his attention to the dossier in front of him and his head of security, sitting across from him, a man in his forties who looked ten years younger and could still take down a twenty-year-old without batting an eyelid.

"Are you sure about this, Khaya?" he asked. "It wasn't an accident?"

"Yes, Sire, I'm sure," General Khaya said. "The collision appears to be an accident. Wrong place, wrong time. However, the car's tires were definitely tampered with to orchestrate the blowout."

Omar swore as anger ballooned inside him, along with a side order of guilt. He shouldn't have put stock in the semblance of peace that had reigned for the past eight months since neutralising the royal family's biggest opposition. Unlike Majid whose mistrust of people had become second nature, Omar still believed in the general good of people.

During his time in the army, he'd seen the best and worst of humanity. Instead of becoming disillusioned like some of his colleagues, he'd instead chosen the path of hope.

After his tour of duty, he'd spent years abroad, managing the kingdom's global business interests and amassing considerable wealth for The Crown. During this time, he'd learned the value of diplomacy. Human beings may not be inherently good, but most would choose to be good with enough incentive. Or so he'd thought.

The result? The enemies of the throne had succeeded in laying their hands on the heir of Sudar. He should have been more vigilant, knowing his brother had been busy finalising the details of the alliance as well as the wedding. He'd see to it all responsible were brought to justice if it was the last thing he did.

"What do we know about the people behind it?" he asked, his deathly calm voice belying the rage roiling in his chest.

"Not a lot, Sire," came the less than satisfactory response. "When we captured the Nassiru gang a year ago, we had reason to believe the threat had been neutralised. We've been monitoring their activities."

"Find every last one of their allies," Omar said. "After they taste my brand of justice, they'll desire death, but I won't be so merciful."

"Your Royal Highness, this wasn't the Nassiru gang. Whatever survived our raid won't have the resources to pull off something like this. It was too seamless."

Omar sensed hesitation in Khaya's answer.

"What are you not telling me?"

"Sire, I believe whoever did this had help."

"What about the driver of the other vehicle?"

"Still in a coma, and it doesn't look good. He wasn't wearing a seatbelt, so we have to assume it was unrelated, or he intended to commit suicide. We don't know whether his motivation was of a personal or religious nature."

He swore. His father had spent a great deal of resources to create opportunities for the youth of

Sudar precisely to keep them from wandering into the hands of people with extremist agendas. Was this evidence of failure? Or just an outlier who'd fallen through the cracks?

"We ran his prints through our database, but it yielded no results. None of our allies have been able to identify him."

"Any other suspects?"

"No, Sire."

"Find me one," Omar barked. "Until you do, I'll need daily updates on your investigation."

"Yes, Sire."

"I also want a list of everyone who had access to the car that day."

"Of course, Sire."

"If there's nothing else, you may go. Please inform Waheed I'll be driving myself to the hospital today."

"Sire?" Khaya said, drawing Omar's attention. "May I ask what arrangements are in place for after Her Royal Highness is discharged from the hospital?"

"She comes home." He raised his brows. "What is it, Khaya?"

"The would-be queen may want to go home to Bagumi and seek the support of her family."

Omar shook his head. "I can't guarantee her safety if I let her leave my protection, so unless I'm able to travel with her, she's going to stay here in Sudar."

Khaya nodded, seemingly satisfied with the response. "A wise decision, Sire."

With that, the head of security bowed and exited the room.

Alone again, Omar pondered Khaya's question, wondering if he should have probed further. When it came to India, it seemed his mind didn't function as well as it usually did, while other parts of his anatomy operated on overdrive.

He checked the time on his phone. *Five o'clock.* Time to wrap up at the office and head over to visit her at the hospital.

His Inherited Princess by Empi Baryeh is out now.

*

Carry on reading to find out more about the next book in the Royal House of Saene series.

BLURB: His Captive Princess by Kiru Taye

Isha Saene has perfected the act of balancing her life—a celebrated corporate negotiator spearheading an international trade deal that could catapult her country to one of the fastest growing mid-sized economies in Africa, and a loyal First Princess of Bagumi Kingdom set to seal ties with a neighbouring nation through marriage.

Until one careless moment knocks her carefully choreographed life into chaos.

Zain Bassong has always fought for the underdog—a patriot dedicated to fighting against the oppression of his people by the country's elite. He believes the pen is mightier than the sword and chooses the diplomatic route, no matter how many times he is arrested by the repressive regime.

Until devastating news triggers a chain reaction.

Isha and Zain are thrown together and their lives change. For better or worse? They will have to figure that out before it's too late.

EXCERPT: His Captive Princess by Kiru Taye

"Mr Bassong, if you will, please arrange for a phone to be sent to me. I would like to rest now. You are dismissed."

He burst out laughing, a cold, echoing mirth that didn't reach his eyes and chilled her to the bones.

As quickly as it started the laughter died and he took a step in her direction.

Her impulse was to step back but she hadn't done anything impulsive in years. She stayed where she stood as he advanced.

"First Princess Isha Ruby—"

"Don't call me that!" Isha couldn't stop the visceral response or the vehemence in her voice when he used her middle name. Her gut wrenched and the throbbing returned to her temple.

He jerked back and raised one dark brow.

"Is that not your name, Ruby Bagumi?" The tone of his voice baited her and his rigid posture mocked her.

She stiffened her spine and squared her shoulders. "You know very well that I am the First Princess of Bagumi Kingdom and my given name is Isha Saene. You can address me as Your Highness or Princess Isha."

"Oh." He tilted his head and scratched the hair on his chin. "Ten years ago, I met a student in London. She was beautiful, intelligent, compassionate, or at least I'd thought she was at the time. She had these brilliant ideas that could change the world. She told me her name was Ruby Bagumi. But I found out it was a lie."

He cut her open with his words, a thousand paper-cuts, making her bleed from her soul.

She closed her eyes tight and balled her fists.

She would not go there, would not bleed for him to see.

I am First Princess Isha Saene, she recited in her mind. Isha Saene.

"I am First Princess Isha Saene," she said out loud and took a deep breath as she opened her eyes.

He stood close. If she reached out she could place her palm on this chest. Was his heart thumping as hard as hers? His scent clung in the air, sandalwood and citrus, tantalising her with each breath.

Memories she'd locked away hovered, threatening to break free.

Nails biting into her palms, she took a step back. "I demand a phone call."

"So that's the way you want to play it." He nodded, moving away as he made his proclamation. "First Princess Isha Saene of the Kingdom of Bagumi, you are now a captive of the MLG group. You will remain in our custody until our demands are met. As for your demand—" he spat out the word as if it was offensive "—you have no power and no rights here. This is Wanai where the supreme power remains with the supreme leader and in this region, I am the supreme leader. You will do as you are told while you are here."

"I will not," she retorted, bristling that he dared to make such a declaration. "I do not submit to your leadership. The only authorities I recognise are my father, His Majesty the King of Bagumi and Almighty God."

He gave that cold laughter again, the one that sent shivers down her spine.

"You are engaged to a Wanaian man. What do you think will happen after you are wed? In Wanai, your husband will have total authority over you."

Her chin jutted as she glared at him. "Kweku and anyone else will be out of their freaking minds if they think I'm going to abide by that antiquated edict."

Her mother would blanch in horror if she had heard Isha speak in this manner. Language suited only to commoners. Still, this man made her forget herself and her upbringing every time.

"There she is. There is the woman I once knew as Ruby Bagumi." For the first time, a small smile tugged the corner of his lips. "Welcome to Wanai. Make yourself comfortable, well, as comfortable as you can under the circumstances. I'll see you again soon."

He whirled around and was gone before she could respond.

Her chest heaved as she tried to catch her breath and make sense of what just happened.

Why was Zain doing this to her? Why was he set on resurrecting the past?

OTHER BOOKS BY LOVE AFRICA PRESS

Healing His Medic by Nana Prah

Queer and Sexy Collection Volume 1 by Eniitan

His Inherited Princess by Empi Baryeh

His Captive Princess by Kiru Taye

Bound To Liberty by Kiru Taye

CONNECT WITH US

Facebook.com/LoveAfricaPress

Twitter.com/LoveAfricaPress

Instagram.com/LoveAfricaPress

www.loveafricapress.com

LOVE AFRICA
PRESS
African Love Stories

CPSIA information can be obtained
at www.ICGtesting.com
Printed in the USA
LVHW091440131019
633942LV00008B/369/P

9 781916 475557